MW00526432

WE ARE WOODSTOCK

by G. A. Eldridge

WE ARE WOODSTOCK

Experienced by G. A. Eldridge

Trivia King Publishing
8212 Braewick
Houston, Texas 77074

Orders: www.WeAreWoodsock.com

For questions or comments email:
info@WeAreWoodstock.com

ISBN 978-0-9829950-1-3

First Edition 2016

Dedications

I dedicate this book to my mother,
Hilda Eldridge.
She always said,
I should write a love story.

I dedicate this book to my father,
Teddy Eldridge.
He always said,
my mother was his love story.

I dedicate this book to my brother,
Thomas Eldridge.
He was serving in the military,
while I was at Woodstock.

- G. A. Eldridge

TABLE OF CONTENTS

ACKNOWLEDGEMENT

Many thanks:

To Jodi Karren, for her support and encouragement.

To Debbie Lazarov, for helping with the written word, as well as, telling me where a comma goes, and for all her tremendous feedback.

To Robert Shniderson, a good friend and a very talented graphic designer, wowing me with the cover and continuing to impress me with his artistic brilliance.

- G. A. Eldridge

ABOUT THE AUTHOR

Glenn A. Eldridge was born in 1950 and grew up in the Bronx, New York. He had various jobs, from working in a drug store and a supermarket to selling soda pop at Yankee Stadium. He also worked at Vanguard Records. He went to college in Alamosa, Colorado for a year and then moved back to New York. During the summer of '69, he worked in the kitchen at Cejwin Camp, in up-state New York. That was the summer of the original Woodstock Festival, which he did attended. He became an apprentice to his father's tin ceiling business and in 1978 moved himself and the business to Houston, Texas, where he now manufactures tin ceilings and distributes them throughout the world. The company name is Chelsea Decorative Metal Company and he is known as "The Tinman."

His love of Rock & Roll music was cultivated in New York City, where he went to many concerts. His first concert was The Doors (featuring Jim Morrison) at the Fillmore East. He saw many musical artists there and was present at the live recording of The Allman Brothers Band. He saw The Who perform, for the first time in this counrty, their rock opera, *Tommy*.

He filled his summers by going to many free concerts at Central Park, where, one time, he actually drank Sangria behind the outdoor stage with Jack Cassady, Jorma and Grace Slick, members of the Jefferson Airplane. He also saw Todd Rundgren perform and he can be seen on the back cover of "Todd" in an audience shot. Greenwich Village was another hot spot for musicians and he met Frank Zappa, when Zappa was doing his "Absolutely Free" show, which, by the way, was not absolutely free.

He attended George Harrison's Concert for Bangladesh, John Lennon's One to One Concert, and Paul MacCartney's Wings Over America show. Sorry to say he never saw the Beatles collectively, but was at the live recording of Elvis at Madison Square Garden, which was another hot spot for many R & R heroes. The lists of artists he's seen is endless.

As a youngster, he always dabbled in writing poetry. Some published in less than prestigest places, in a camp newsletter and a school bulletin news. He wrote a couple of short stories.

In 2008 he had a reading of a play called, *The Many Loves of Bert.* In 2011 he self-published, *The $5,000 Trivia Treasure Hunt Challenge.* Most recently he had a reading of a ten minute play, *The Mysterious Room*, which he's has submitted to a 10 x 10 festival for consideration. But of all his accomplishments, Glenn is most proud to say he is the father of his two daughters.

This story is considered a historical fiction love story with some autobiographical material thrown in. This book has taken two years to write, forty-seven years in the making, and is Glenn's newest endeavor. This is his first novel, *We are Woodstock.*

PROLOGUE:
Woodstock History

I appreciate that you're reading my book and will accompany me on this visit back to Woodstock, which originally took place August 15th-17th 1969. The weekend I remember, or at least I think I remember, is true. The joke has always been, "If you remember Woodstock, you weren't there." That is based on the fact that there was sex, drugs, and Rock & Roll. Today the saying should be, "If you remember Woodstock, you have a great memory since you are old and on your last leg." For it's over 47 years ago when the hippies of Woodstock had the best time of their lives. I was there, I remember. It was the best time in my life and why wouldn't it be, there was sex, drugs and Rock & Roll. Strangely that's all I can remember of these days. Most of my memory is based on the fact that I have told the stories over and over again. Is it fact? It was once said in a movie, I saw, *The Man that Shot Liberty Valance*, that "When the legend becomes fact, print the legend." This story should be considered historical fiction, and I will take you back there myself, to the Woodstock Festival, the way it was on that weekend back in August, 1969.

First, I want to assure all you readers that I was truly there. Everyone has a story, and, as well, I have mine, but I also have 47 years on top of that. That means I can look back on Woodstock, but I can also look forward from it. The bulk of the story takes place from August 14, just one day before the start of the festival until August 18, one day after the festival was suppose to end, with a few detours through the future thrown in.

My book is as much about my generation as it is about a wonderful weekend. Nearly everyone in the world has heard about Woodstock. When I meet people and tell them I was there, I seem to sense a hint of jealousy, but at the same time it tells the person more about me than I can explain. It's never hindered me when meeting people. It was a weekend of growing up, and I know it changed my life.

It wasn't Woodstock that made that weekend famous; it's the people that made Woodstock famous. You need to know that. Everyone came for the music, wanting to see the groups that sang the songs that made up our lives, the songs played on the radio, on our turntables, in our ears and emitted from our souls. We came to Yasgur's farm as individuals with the same belief, that the world can be a better place with love and music. It turned out to be the biggest and best party one could ever go to, a place in the American music world that brought attention to my generation. I'm happy to have been at Woodstock. It's this farm, this party, and this concert to end all concerts that will be the background to a love story, my love story.

Before we take the journey back let me explain why Woodstock. The town of Woodstock, New York, was established in 1787, and through the late 1800s various painters from many schools would come to Woodstock. In the early 1900s an Arts and Crafts Movement came to Woodstock, and it became known as an Artist Colony. I have found that one of the major groups was Hervey White's Maverick Art Colony, and from 1915 through 1931, they held the Maverick Festival each summer where people turned out for art, theater, music, and lots of partying. Let's flash forward to the 1960s, where the likes of Richie Havens, Paul Butterfield, Bob Dylan and The Band, and even Janis Joplin would turn out to play. I mention these to show the caliber of musicians that were in the area and other than Bob Dylan the others all played at the Woodstock Festival.

It was this town's reputation that inspired the promoters to have their music festival in this area and call it the Woodstock Music and Art Fair, but I found that their plan was squashed when the town turned down their request for permits. Ouch! That site was Mills Industrial Park in Wallkill, New York, and the rejection to the permits was based on some cockamamie reason that the port-a-potties wouldn't meet the town's code. I would say, "That's a lot of shit." Michael Lang had expected 50,000 people although at a time closer to the concert, he projected 200,000 people. Still wrong.

Michael found and got in touch with Max Yasgur, who had a 600-acre dairy farm. They met, they talked, and they agreed on a price of $75,000, which was ten times more than they had been expecting to pay at the other site. Max was no dummy. This price surely helped Max, since it hadn't been a very profitable year so far.

I actually agree with Michael's choice, he couldn't have found a better spot to hold this festival because of the contour of the land, especially the bowl-shaped field where the concert itself was held. So now that you know about the farm, let me review for you the players. If you really want to learn more about them and their roles, you can read their books, but here is a synopsis.

John Roberts and Joel Rosenman were very much the Ivy-league, preppy type of guys. John was the heir to the Polident Denture Cream fortune and grew up in New Jersey. He graduated from the University of Pennsylvania in 1966 and looked like he came out of a Brooks Brothers commercial.

Strangely enough Joel Rosenman was the son of a dentist and grew up in Long Island. He graduated from Princeton and went on to also graduate from the Yale Law School. John and Joel met in 1966 and became such good friends that they moved in together in New York City.

They quit their jobs a year later to do their own venture together and found themselves with a proposal to build a recording studio in Manhattan. They opened the studio under the name Media Sound on 57th Street and 8th Avenue, and it became very popular, so by 1968 they found themselves very much in the music business.

They were inspired to take out an ad in *The Wall Street Journal* that read, "YOUNG MEN WITH UNLIMITED CAPITAL looking for interesting legitimate investment opportunities and business propositions. X1739 Times."

3

Michael Lang and Artie Kornfeld were very much on a completely different track than John and Joel, not even in the same train station. Michael left his home in Brooklyn at 16 and later dropped out of NYU. He moved to Florida and opened one of the first head shops in Miami. He also promoted rock bands and would put on small rock festivals.

Artie was also born in Brooklyn, but by 1968 he was already in the music field having written over 30 songs. He was also a producer and the vice president of Capitol Records.

At the end of 1968 Michael had moved up north in the back woods of the Woodstock area and was managing a group. When he called Capitol Records to discuss the group, he and Artie found out they were from the same neighborhood, so Artie sets up an appointment. They, like John and Joel, quickly became friends and both came up with an idea of a festival to help kick-start a recording studio, which Michael thought was needed at Woodstock. There were many musicians there as I mentioned earlier, so it seemed like a great retreat where artists could record.

Michael and Artie wanted their own recording studio while John and Joel had already established one in New York City. Miles Lourie, a lawyer who had dealt with all four of them, called Joel to sent up a meeting. When the two hippies walked in, that being Michael and Artie, John and Joel were taken aback. The original proposal was slapped down on the table, but what John was intrigued by was what he read at the bottom of the proposal, which stated something similar to this, "Since there are many musicians living up in Woodstock we think we can get some to do a concert for the opening of the studio." John and Joel had this great idea to have the concert first to generate funds for the recording studio. Since the Monterey Pop Festival had been only 18 months earlier and the movie of that event was just released during the Christmas of 1968, in John's mind he thought, "We'll have another Monterey Pop Festival." There you have it, the *Reader's Digest* version of how Woodstock, the greatest Rock & Roll Festival of all time, got started.

4

So in even a briefer summation, John Roberts and Joel Rosenman had the money. Artie Kornfeld, more the speaker and Michael Lang, more the hippie-looking guy, had the idea to start a recording studio. They collaborated with the moneymen and planned a concert to introduce the studio to musicians, but then decide on a festival first. Snow-balling from there, Woodstock is born. It was these four men that were considered the promoters of the Woodstock Music and Art Fair that registered the name Woodstock Ventures Inc. They made history.

Artie Kornfeld is known as The Father of Woodstock. Artie is considered responsible for signing up the groups, some even signed just before going on stage and credited for hiring the award winning director Michael Wadleigh to shoot the film. As I have learned since then, he is also credited with playing a big role in stopping development on Yasgur's farm after Max sold it. He is the writer of the book, *The Pied Piper of Woodstock*.

Michael Lang, who has now been introduced to you, is considered half the developer of the concept of a major festival, which he did with Artie Kornfeld. Michael helped find the site. As I have learned since then, he produced Woodstock 94 and Woodstock 99, anniversaries of the original 1969 Woodstock. He is the writer of the book, *The Road to Woodstock*.

Joel Rosenman and John Roberts were the financial investors. Joel is involved with investments and financing. John, I'm sorry to say, died from cancer in 2001 at the age of 56. Their book is *Young Men with Unlimited Capital: The Inside Story of the Legendary Woodstock Festival Told by the Two People Who Paid for It.*

August 14, 1969 (Thursday)
CHAPTER 1: The Journey Begins

The 1960s were a time of turmoil with the assassination of President John F. Kennedy and Martin Luther King; also a time when challenges were met head-on, as was the landing on the moon and the passing of the Civil Rights Act. There were great times too, The Beatles appeared, the music revolution exploded and the Hippie Counter Culture Movement was created. The Sixties brought a time of conflict and unity. Conflict took the form of The Vietnam War, while unity took the form of the Woodstock Festival. This particular story is my coming of age story and where it took place was at the Woodstock Festival.

It's almost 4:00 p.m. on Thursday, August 14, 1969, when we get to Woodstock, a day before the concert is scheduled to begin. We find ourselves at a campground parking lot, very close to the area of the concert where we are hoping to set up camp. We park between two buses that are still unloading hippies, like ourselves, who are carrying camping gear similar to what we brought. We unload and haul our backpacks, sleeping bags, a cooler and a box filled with food, our canteens, our tent and a five lb. can of baked beans. Oh, and maybe some drugs, but I don't wish to incriminate myself. I expect there will be many more hippies coming, but who could tell how many. Right now there are three of us, Brian, Sam and me. I'm Glenn.

Let me first tell you about Brian. He is a thin guy; his belt has an extra hole so he can tighten it enough to hold up his jeans. He wears a T-shirt most of the time and the T-shirts are usually tie-dye, which he makes himself. His brown hair is parted dead center and runs straight down to his armpits, while his matching mustache runs across his face and looks like it connects the left side of his hair with the right side. His semi-dark sunglasses aren't prescription, but he wears them all the time, whether it's morning, noon or night. He grew up in the same neighborhood as me, and went to the same school. The three of us planned this trip together even though I had to work for the summer and they didn't. They have been staying at Sam's family home, which is upstate. I purposely got a job upstate so they could pick me up when this weekend came.

Sam also went to the same school, but is a much closer friend of Brian, than he is to me, but we all get along great. Sam is a much huskier guy and lovable like a teddy bear. His hair is reddish brown in an Afro style that covers his ears. He loves to wear a sheepskin vest all the time. It's soft on the inside and has some colorful print on the outside and he wears it with or without a shirt depending on how he feels or if he has a clean shirt or not. He also wears blue sunglasses, but not all the time.

As for me, I wear prescription glasses with plain clear glass. My hair is like Brian's, straight, but not as long, and it's black, pitch black. I wear a bandana all the time and that helps control my hair. I usually wear a button down, rolled up long sleeve flowery shirts, but it looks like they only brought my T-shirts. I wear jeans all the time, but not always blue denim, sometimes orange, sometimes khaki and sometimes a bright blue. If you ever saw the Levi man commercials, he would zap the figures wearing plain white clothes into colorful clothes; well, I was the one that got zapped. The three of us don't look that much different than the hippies of our generation. So here we are, on a farm on the outskirts of Bethel, New York, looking for a place to pitch our tent, but let me digress to earlier this day.

Today finally arrives, and I'm gonna take off work for a few days with my girlfriend, Sharon. We had been dating since we first met at the beginning of the summer and today we will be heading up to Bethel with a couple of my friends, who were coming to pick us up.

I purchased my ticket when they first went on sale eight months ago. Back then, the concert was to be held at Wallkill, New York, and the list of artists was staggering and spewing out like a list of Who's Who in the record industry. I don't wish to bore you with the names of the artists now because they will be forthcoming in the next few days, and besides, I have a much bigger development to share with you since you are taking this journey with me.

I'd been working for the summer at Camp Cejwin, a nice Zionistic sleep-overnight camp in Port Jervis. I'd been a camper there when I was young, but now I was working in the kitchen. They originally didn't want me to work here because I was Jewish, and a Jew shouldn't work in the kitchen, according to them, but I explained that I really needed a job for the summer, so they hired me. At that time, I had arranged with my boss to have this weekend off to go to Wallkill to attend "The Woodstock Music & Art Fair: 3 Days of Peace & Music."

On July 15 the Zoning Board of Appeals at Wallkill banned the concert. The promoters, known as Woodstock Ventures Inc., only had a month to find a new location since the concert was scheduled for August 15-17. There was a dairy farmer named Max Yasgur who had 600 acres of land and with time running out there really wasn't much of a choice, but it would prove to be an excellent location. So the land was leased, and the new location at Bethel was announced, just 45 miles from my summer job.

Today I go to my boss to inform him I'm leaving for the weekend.

"Hi Boss, just letting you know I'm checking out and heading up north."

"Where do you think you're going?" he questioned.

"Remember, when I started working here, I asked you for this weekend off, so I can go to a concert in Wallkill? Well, now it's being held in Bethel."

"You can't go!" he said.

"Well, I got my ticket and I—"

"I said you couldn't go," he interrupted in a harsh voice, "you're needed here, and if you leave now, don't show your face around here again."

It turned out there were still a couple of weeks left to work, but I wasn't gonna miss this festival. I had planned on coming back afterwards, but he wasn't giving me an option. So I simply turn towards the door and said, "Goodbye!"

"Wait! Wait! When can you get back here?"

His tone was quite different, it sounded a bit desperate.

"I was planning on coming back Sunday afternoon," I said.

"Okay, alright! That's fine," he said.

"But now, I won't be coming back at all, "Goodbye again!"

I turned to the door and headed to the kitchen where Sharon should be finishing up. It's almost 2:15 p.m., and since lunchtime was over, the kitchen should be clean by now.

"Sharon, are you ready to leave?"

"No!" she answered.

"I'll wait for you, just hurry up."

"I'm not going."

"Why not?" I asked.

"I'm breaking up with you," she informed me.

"But, We, I, What?"

"I'm breaking up with you because you're so immature. I'm going out with someone else, and I'm not interested in you or your childish festival."

She had been my girlfriend for about six weeks, and I wanted us to enjoy the festival together before the summer ended. I was blindsided and never thought it would end like this. I must have been naïve. I never saw it coming. I was hurt, but also too excited to let this stop me. I'm sure it will hit me later. Maybe Ken, another friend can go, I thought.

"Well, Sharon I'm stunned and disappointed, but maybe you can give your ticket to Ken, so he can come with me?"

"No! I don't think so because that's who I'm dating now."

"That sucks," I said. "I'll just have to have a good time without you."

I don't know what possessed me to grab a five lb. can of baked beans from the pantry on my way out, but it was like, "Oh, yeah! Well, let this teach you a lesson, I'm taking the beans." Not much of a statement, but to hell with her and Ken, and while I'm at it, to hell with my boss.

So I left with this can of beans and waited outside for Brian and Sam to pick me up. I took out my red bandana, which I never wore at work, and put it on. Within minutes Brian with Sam drove up. I got in the car and we were off.

"Where's your girlfriend," Brian asked.

"It seems my Barbie found another Ken," I answered. "Did

you guys bring all my stuff?"

"I think we got it all," Sam said, "but it looks like you brought something extra."

"Yeah, I grabbed this can of beans."

Now we were on our way to Bethel, by way of Highway I-87, not knowing that in a couple of days from now, Arlo Guthrie would be making the announcement that, "The New York State Throughway is closed, man!" Which would be true. Well, it would be partly true. You see the highway would be closed to anybody coming to Woodstock, but the roads were open if you wanted to leave, but I'm sure no one was gonna leave, at least not for the next few days. So there we were on the road to history, and we didn't even know it.

Now that we've caught up, I can continue from here. We are at Yasgur's farm, walking down this pebble road from the car, and when we reach the grass, there is sort of a path on it formed by the many people who have already arrived. As we walk with our camping gear, we come to a fork in the road where there are several intersections, and the paths have already been named. According to three hand-painted signs nailed to a tree, their names are High Way, Gentle Path, and Groovy Way. Groovy Way seems to lead to a dead end, so we choose this path to set up our tent. We walk down the path, and it has people setting up tents on either side. We smile, nod, and greet our friendly neighbors until we stop to pitch our tent at the first available space.

A little further down the trail, at the dead-end of the path, is a pipe sticking out of the ground, horizontally, about a foot and a half high with clean, clear, drinkable water streaming out. I don't know where it's coming from or why it's here, but it's a private little watering hole for us and the other campers who now reside on Groovy Way.

We start making the acquaintance of our fellow campers and meet three travelers who have driven all the way from Oregon and two couples who have driven down from Calgary. They met somewhere during their route, and since they were all coming to Woodstock, they followed each other here and have decided to set up their tents next to each other.

The air is filled with a pungent smell that is familiar to me, but I'm not partaking just yet since we still need to set up our tent and get the sleeping bags situated. It's great to be here, but I'm starting to think about Sharon and how I got dumped. I really hope it won't haunt me this weekend, so before it does, I quickly erase her from my mind.

Once we settle in, I decide to check out the surroundings. To the side of Groovy Way is a cornfield, which I walk alongside until I get to the end, where I can clearly see the stage that is being built just past the open field that will soon seat the audience. The ground in front of me drops downward suddenly, so if I were to sit here my feet would dangle down just reaching the lower ground, from there the ground levels off and gradually descends all the way down to the stage. The grass has been beautifully mowed, making this the perfect place for a large outdoor concert. This slight plateau I'm standing on runs in front of the cornfield on the side that faces the stage and is a beautiful spot to sit and watch everything, but we'll look for a better place tomorrow somewhere we can lay down blankets.

I look out towards the enormous stage with its gigantic platform, about 80 feet long made of blonde wood planks held up on orange metal supports maybe 15 to 20 feet high in the back where the ground keeps sloping, but in the front of the stage that faces the spectators its only about 6-8 feet high from the ground. Other planks lay around the platform, not yet put in their proper place, as workers move around, some slowly and others swiftly. Other orange supports make up the scaffolding that tower high above the stage on either side, and there are six scaffolds in all. Cranes soar even higher, standing behind the scaffolding. One crane is lifting a huge spotlight to place on one of the landing on the scaffoldings. In the far distance, behind this mammoth sight, is a lake. I look out on the landscape as the sun's shining over the land and is heading down in the western sky. I'm enjoying the serenity that is broken only by the faint echoes of the hammering as the carpenters continue working.

Suddenly, a loud, non-harmonious sound of a motorcycle hurts my ears. It's speeding down the grass towards the stage. I recognize, from pictures I've seen, that it's Michael Lang with his bushy, afro-style hair. He's one of the organizers of the festival, and although I would praise him for this enormous undertaking, right now he's disturbing the tranquility I'm basking in, so I head back to the campsite that I will call home for the next few days.

I approach Groovy Way, and the familiar smell is stronger, yet sweeter than before. I find my friends, and as we eat some grub, the sun is disappearing for the night. Once we finish eating, we go over and sit down on the ground to watch a bunch of flower children dancing around a huge bonfire to the music of a flute, a bongo, and a guitar. Brian lights up a joint so we can finally get high as I'm keeping the beat to the music with my foot as I watch the free-spirited dancers rotate clockwise around the blaze. They're turning around and throwing their hands in the air; it's a tribal dance to the Fire God. Then, one of the girls dancing catches my eye because she's so pretty.

She's on the opposite side of the fire, but I can see her face clearly lit up by the glow coming from the flames. She has on a headband that tries to hold her hair in place, but fails; her hair flies across her shoulders and around her neck and into the air as she swings her head about to the music. Her cheeks are smooth, and the orange hue from the fire reflects off them. Her eyebrows match her brown hair and hang over her eyes that are evenly placed on either side of her cute, little nose, and her tongue moistens her lips as I watch.

As she starts to come around the fire, I can see her body gyrating to the rhythm of the flute. She's wearing an off-white peasant dress that comes down right below her knees. Her head spins in my direction and then away. She's directly between the fire and me with her back towards me. I can see the outline of her body through the thin, white fabric of her dress, which allows me to gaze at her symmetrical body. I can see the curve of her hips and her slender legs and the nice fit of her panties. As she circles around to the left side of the blaze, I can see the front of her dress and the bangles on her wrists. Her hands brush her hair down as her dress slightly flies up freely with every swinging movement of her hips. She's so exciting to watch, I can't take my eyes off her. Brian and Sam are to my right, and Brian nudges me, and I turn towards him, taking the joint he's offering and quickly turn back.

As I turn back towards her, she's once again on the far side of the fire, but is facing away from the heat and the light smoke that is floating upward. She's coming around to the right side again, and her hips give a quick half turn that makes her dress spread upward and outward flaring up slightly again. I can see the passion in her every step. Again, she dances between the luminous luster of the campfire light and me, but this time she's half turned, and I can see the profile of her face, and through her garment I can see the silhouette of her breasts. She's not wearing a bra, and they stick firmly out with a slight jiggle that I can't miss because I'm so intently connecting with her dancing, but mostly because I'm just plain staring. Brian takes the joint back as I see the flickering light from the flames on the front of her dress, and she's now on the left side of the fire again. Her head is moving up and down to the beat of the bongo, and then the beat of the bongo stops. The guitar and the flute stop and she stops, looking directly at me, she smiles for a second or two, and then looks away as the amateur musicians start again. I frantically think to myself, I didn't smile back, I should have smiled back, why didn't I smile back? I'll tell you why I didn't smile back; her look took me by surprise. I was too busy admiring her beauty, her motion, and her body that I didn't expect she would look at me, let alone smile at me. I continue to watch her.

14

She's back to dancing on the far side of the fire, and I look at her through the floating embers and the jaggedness of the high flames. She looks straight at me again, but this time I smile at her, a great big smile. Then I see the corners of her lips quickly lift up into a huge smile back, and then her head turns away. She's coming around the right side again, reaching for the sky as she swirls, and I can't help but anticipate her dancing on this side of the fire again, bringing her close to me. Now she's in front of the fire again, but facing me, all I want to do is look into her eyes, which I can't because the light from the flame is behind her, and there's a shadow masking her face. I smile in her direction hoping she's looking at me. Brian nudges me again. I hesitantly take the joint, inhale, and then hand it back, but as I turn to the ritual again I don't see her anymore. She's gone. I lean forward to look for her, I look at each and every dancer, but I don't see her. I even stand up, but no sight of her, so I sit back down and think, "Where the hell did she go?" Even though she's gone, I think to myself, "It really doesn't get much better than this." Then, all of a sudden, she sits down next to me with a lit joint in her mouth. Well, maybe it does.

CHAPTER 2: Gail

She finishes puffing on the joint and offers it to me, which I graciously take from her hand. I take a nice big hit, hold in the smoke, and try to hand it back, but she motions to pass it the other way. As I exhale the smoke in Brian's direction, I hand it to him, so now he has two joints. I turn to her with a smile and say,

"Hi, I was watching you dance. You really have some nice moves."

"I noticed you watching me," she says. "What's your name?"

"Oh! I'm sorry. I'm Glenn, and you're . . .?"

I stuck out my hand, and she shakes it.

"I'm Gail."

"Gale, like a bird, a nightingale. I can see that. I watched as you reached up to the sky with your wings and your hair waving. You have such beautiful hair, and it was swirling exquisitely around your head as you danced gracefully about the fire, almost taking flight into the heavens."

"Do you always talk like this when you're high?" she asks.

"I don't know. I don't really listen to myself."

"You're funny," she says, "but I believe you probably talk like that when you're high."

"I don't think I've gotten high off that one hit."

"I saw you smoking before, but yes, you can get that high off one hit of my stuff. You must be high, I can't believe you talk like that any other way."

"Ah! Maybe. Were you watching me?" I ask.

"Yes!" Gail says. "I told you I was watching you. I was watching you watching me."

"Oh! I know you were watching, I mean, I was watching you. Wait! We were watch . . . Okay! Yeah, your stuff is good. I'm pretty high right now, but I was smoking before you sat down. Oh! You know that. Anyway you said your name is Gale like the bird, right?"

"Well, not exactly," she explains, "the truth is that gale is like a strong wind, so I would be more like a hurricane than a bird except for one thing."

"And what would that be?" I question.

"I don't spell it like the wind, G-A-L-E, but Gail, G-A-I-L, which means 'joy' in Hebrew."

"Do you know Hebrew?" I ask. "Are you Jewish?"

"No . . . and yes."

The joint comes back, and I pass it directly to Gail. She takes a hit and passes it on its merry way in the other direction.

Then I ask,

"Are we in a utopia, where life is peaceful, and we share food, drink, and smoke?"

"No! It just seems that way because you're high."

"You keep saying, 'I'm high,' but I don't think so. Wait! I admitted to being high before, didn't I? Ah! What did I ask you about before, that you answered yes, no or no, yes? I forget."

"I forgot too," she says.

Then we both start laughing.

"Didn't you say something about me having beautiful hair?" she inquires.

"Did I? Did I say that? I'm not sure I might have?"

She suddenly moves her face close to mine and in a hushed voice, asks, "Do you think I have beautiful hair?"

"Well, yeah."

"Then you must have said it because I remember hearing it."

"Yeah, you do have beautiful hair, and yeah, I probably said it."

Actually, I don't remember if I said it or not.

We sway to the music while watching the other flower children continue to dance around the flames. I don't know how many times the joint past back and forth or how much wine we drank, but we are pretty stoned. When I turn to Gail, she turns towards me like she's waiting for me to say something. I just want to look at her because of her beauty and not because I have something to say. The longer I look, the more she waits for me to say something, and then I finally do,

"He plays a mean bongo."

"But he's nothing without her flute," she says back.

"I like your dress," I say, searching for another topic.

"It's just something light and airy, and that's how I feel tonight."

I just smile, probably that goofy smile I have when I'm stoned. Her brown hair hangs straight down from under her headband, and when she turns to face me, I can only see half her face lit up by the campfire, while the other half's hidden in the darkness of her own shadow. Even half her face looks lovely. Why don't I just tell her that? I told her about her hair, I think.

"Where are you from?" I ask.

"San Francisco. I flew in this morning, and we drove here today. It was a wonderful ride, and the trees are so colorful. I've never been this far east before."

I didn't see a "we," and I didn't ask.

"And you?"

"I'm from the Bronx, that's just north of New York City, but I'm working . . . I mean, I was working in Port Jervis about 45 miles away. I had to quit my job to come here because my boss wouldn't give me the time off."

"You quit your job? What did you do?" she asks.

"I just walked out."

"No!" she said smiling. "What was your job?"

"Oh! I worked in a kitchen, cleaning the dishes and the big mixing machines. I also hosed down the floors and mats and put everything away. It was at a camp. What do you do in San Francisco?"

"Me? I'm a stripper."

"Oh! (Pause) You have the body for it."

Why did I say that, I ask myself.

"Do you really think so? I saw you watching it."

I wonder if she knows how much of her body I was watching, but I guess if she's a stripper, it doesn't really matter. I wasn't sure what to say next, I was at a loss for words, but maybe she senses that because she continues,

"No, You Silly, I'm not a stripper, but it's nice to know you think I can be . . . I think. I just finished school, and I'm planning to go to college, just not sure where I want to go and not sure what I want to do."

"I'm sure you'll be successful at whatever you do, even if it involves stripping," I say.

"You're sweet, but I pray it doesn't involve that. Come with me," she urges.

She gets up and reaches for my hand to help pull me up. I'm hoping she doesn't have us dancing around the fire, but I will if she wants. Instead, she leads me into the cornfield. We enter between the rows of corn stalks that stand tall above our heads.

"I can't see much," I say. "Its kind of dark in here."

"That's why I wanted you to come with me. "Wait here!"

She walks about eight or so steps ahead, and I can barely make out her figure because of the darkness.

"What are you doing?" I ask.

"Don't worry," she says, "it won't take me long."

I hear a slight rustling and can make out that she's squatting.

"I have to pee," she says.

"That's a great idea."

I step a few feet further away from her, and I go also. I don't know how many times I will go in this cornfield this weekend, but I'm sure the corn will be well watered and fertilized too, and not just by me, but by others because I didn't see any bathrooms anywhere.

"Great!" I yell.

"What's the matter?"

"I hit the stalk, and it's splashing back on my feet," I answer. "Stop laughing."

When we are both finished, I lead her through to the opposite end where I stood on the plateau in front of the cornfield earlier this afternoon. When we reach the end of the stalks, we sit down and look out at the field, which is lit up by the moon's light. It's a quarter moon with a crooked smile looking down on us. In the distance, on the anchored stage are lights for the workers. There are also sparks of light from the scaffolding where the workers are welding another spotlight in place, so they can shine the light down on the performers.

"With all the sparks flying," she says, "it looks like a light show."

"Yeah, I saw the sparks earlier, but they look much better at night. I can hardly wait until tomorrow when the concert starts. I've had my ticket forever."

"I don't have a ticket," she informs me.

"You flew all the way here without a ticket?"

"I figured I'd just see what happens when I get here, so far, so good. Actually it's been very good."

Does she mean because of me? Probably not, I mean we just met, but I think tonight is great because of her.

"Look!" Gail points out. "People are already sitting on the lawn in front of the stage."

"There wasn't anybody there earlier."

Then I turn to look at her in the darkness, I can see her face because of the moon.

"Who did you come to see?" I ask.

"I'm a big fan of Melanie and Janis Joplin."

"Just the women artists, huh?"

"No! I like lots of groups too, but definitely both of them. I like Grace Slick, and I think Jimi Hendrix is sexy. What about you, who did you come to see?"

"I really love The Who. I'd have to say they're my favorite group playing this weekend. I've never seen them, but I'm looking forward to it. I've seen some of the other groups."

"Like who?" she asks with excitement.

"The Jefferson Airplane and The Grateful Dead."

"I've seen them too, they're both from San Francisco, you know."

"Yeah, I didn't think of that. I haven't seen Jimi yet, and would very much like too. There's someone here that I really don't know."

"Who's that?"

"Swami Bologna."

"Swami who?"

"Swami Sacagawea or something like that," I say.

"Oh! The Swami. You're funny."

"But otherwise, I think I know most of the groups or at least heard of them, and I'm looking forward to seeing them. Oh yeah! Also Crosby, Stills, Nash and—"

Suddenly she takes her two arms and wraps them around my neck and pulls me in for a very unexpectedly kiss. As our mouths meet I feel her tongue rapidly trying to slip between my lips. I don't separate my lips too wide, but her tongue still manages to push its way into my mouth as my tongue pushes back. Once she's in they begin to wrestle. I put my arms around her and pull her body close to me as she continues hugging my neck. I'm pretty damn high, and it feels pretty damn good. I'm sure it's not taking as long as it feels, but when she finally withdraws her tongue it's a good time to take a breath, and it seems we both need oxygen.

The little light enables me to gaze into her eyes; I assume they're half shut from being high, but between those slits I can see her staring back. I want to say something, but I'm speechless. Who wants to talk now anyway? My arms are around her holding her close. It happened so fast I was taken by surprise, maybe because she didn't know how I would react, but I was definitely accepting, and now she seems to be leaning in for more, but less feverishly.

Our lips touch, and we engage again, but a little more playful now, first in my mouth, and then in hers. We are having fun and I slip out my tongue and give her a little puckered kiss and lean back. She's smiling and the only word I can verbalize is "Wow!" And I verbalize that half out of breath. I find my vision bouncing from her eyes to her nose, to her eyes and her lips, her brow, her cheeks, but always back to those eyes.

"Gail, you're a great kisser, or I'm really, really stoned, or both."

"I can taste the wine in your mouth," she says, and then licks her lips.

"I just need some air," I say.

"Do you want to stop?"

"Yeah."

Even with the slight light in the darkness, I can see a sad and perplexing look on her face.

"Yeah, I want to stop . . . I want to stop talking and continue kissing."

That brings on that smile of hers that I'm getting to like already and she hugs me around the neck tighter and pulls me in for some more smooching. She feels so good in my arms, and I feel like I never wanna let her go.

24

Our bodies mesh together as our kissing continues, and now I can feel the softness of her lips. I lean my weight towards her body, and her back slowly lowers itself down to the grass as her legs stretch outward. I'm lying over her with my whole body, yet our lips never parted. When I stop to take another breath, I lean back and stare down at her face.

"I never knew how important breathing was until now."

"You're funny," she says.

I lower myself down on her and my arms are behind her, so I automatically reach to unclasp her bra through the fabric of her dress, but upon feeling no strap, I remember she isn't wearing a bra. My hands are now beneath her body, and as I try to withdraw them, she leans the weight of her body back, so as to hold my arms in place between her back and the ground. I think she deliberately does this to constrain my hands from the freedom to venture elsewhere. I then go back to focusing on the kissing. I think we stop for air occasionally, but I don't notice it as much now.

Her tongue concentrates more on my lips now than probing between them, and I've never had that done before. My tongue just lays dormant as her tongue licks my lips going around my whole mouth on the outside. It feels good, but it also tickles, and I decide just to enjoy it. It feels unusual, but sexy, and I wonder if she can feel the part of me that is not dormant, but is getting hard and pressing against her leg. I start to wiggle my arms free from behind her, but this time I meet resistance from her upper arms, still holding my arms in place. I'm sure she's doing it intentionally.

Then, we hear other campers approaching from the side of the cornfield, and we stop. We crawl back between the stalks and we can see them, and soon, they will see us. I don't really care, but Gail jumps up quickly and ducks back deeper between the stalks heading back to the campsite with me following. As I catch up with her I grab her arm and pull her back and just hug her. Just simply hug her.

I start thinking that here I'm in the middle of a cornfield, in the middle of a farm, on the outskirts of a town, in the middle of nowhere, with this girl in my arms, and her head leaning into my chest. I hear her breathing, and I feel a ripple down her body when she swallows. Maybe it's because I'm stoned, but I feel I would fall over if I weren't holding her. But at the same time I feel her leaning into me as if she would fall if I weren't here. We are balancing on each other, and if one of us moves, we might both fall down. I'm standing there, looking down the length of the corn stalks, and though my mind is racing, my body remains perfectly still holding on to her. It feels so comfortable and natural holding her. Then, I slowly let her go, and say,

"No one has ever kissed me like you do."

She looks straight at me and says, "No one has ever held me like you do."

Then she stretches forward and upward to kiss me, just a quick one.

"Goodnight," she says.

Then, she scurries back toward the fire, while I'm in a daze after that hug. By the time I reach the end, she's gone. No one is dancing around the fire anymore, and there are very few campers still up. I have no idea which tent she went into, not that it matters. She's gone, and I probably won't see her again, but for now, I decide to go back into the cornfield to finish some unfinished business. Then I head back to my tent where Brian and Sam are already asleep, so I can tuck myself in for the night.

CHAPTER 3: An Aquarian Exposition

You have to realize that the Woodstock Festival is billed as "An Aquarian Exposition." Aquarian comes from the phrase "The Age of Aquarius," and is defined in astrology as spiritual and to bring harmony to earth, while exposition means a large-scale exhibition. I want you to recognize this isn't just a concert, and the 600 acres of Max's land is not just a parking lot. Of course, it's for parking and camping, but there's actually a lot more going on.

There is an area known as the Hog Farm, named after an organized hippie commune whose members were asked by Woodstock Ventures Inc. to help at the festival. They flew in days earlier and helped build fire pits and made walking trails, and they convinced the promoters to have a free-kitchen, which they'd run. That's a nice idea and will turn out to be a great necessity. Not very far from their domain is the Free Stage, where lesser-known acts will perform all weekend long.

The main stage is where all the major acts are scheduled to perform and that's in front of Festival Field. It's also known as The Bowl and that's because it's somewhat curved around on three sides, so erecting the stage at the lowest end made it a perfect outdoor amphitheater. When Michael Lang flew over Yasgur's property in a helicopter, he found this particular area to be very appealing for the Woodstock Concert. All other areas on Yasgur's Farm are relatively level or with a slight grade which makes it excellent for all the surrounding area activities, especially for parking lots and camping grounds, even for just walking around the property.

To the left of the stage as you are watching the concert there are three important sections.

First is the heliport, where the musicians are brought in. The roads are so blocked the performers have to be flown in by helicopters. The second is the Performers Pavilion. This is where the acts stay to eat, sleep, and meet other performers. It's from here they can reach the entrance to the bridge that was built to get them over West Shore Road to the back of the stage which is 15 feet above the ground level. Third is the most important for everybody and that is the medical facility, which is made up of two tents. One tent is the main infirmary for emergencies, while the other can be considered the holding tank for minor injuries and a place for the hippies on bad acid trips to eventually come down. The main tent can be found easily because not only is it the larger tent, it's also pink and white.

If you are taking West Shore Road back towards the highway, which is where people are coming from, and walking away from this stage area, you pass the Security Trailers, more medical tents, an unfinished entrance, and an information booth that can help you find any and all locations throughout the property.

There's a carnival here with a Ferris wheel, that strangely enough I haven't seen. You can also visit the Arts and Craft Fair or the American Indian art exhibit. There's a playground for children and a wooded area. There's a food section that's called "Food for Love," and people have no trouble finding that location because they're set up under high tents, which can be seen on the horizon from The Bowl. The lines there will be very long until the food runs out, and I can tell you that with so many people here, the food will run out soon. There are water stations that have been created, phone lines constructed, and portable toilets set up.

There is one unusual site at this enormous event and that is "Movement City." It stands separate from everything else, as it's on the far side of the wooded area. It's peaceful, but the tent is designated for radical political groups that hand out literature and talk with people. It has its own music and entertainment. Political groups run it, but their relationship with the promoters isn't a popular one, and the groups have done little to even let people know they're here. No signs have been posted or flyers handed out to attract people to their facility.

Many parts are set up as campgrounds, and we are lucky to have gotten here last night, so we could park and set ourselves up at a campsite very near to Festival Field, again, considered The Bowl, which is where the concert will be held.

While we sleep all this property is rapidly filling up with people from all over the world, making Woodstock not only a city, but also one with the second largest population in New York State.

CHAPTER 4: Chip Monck

The day starts early as it always does when camping out. The sun is our silent alarm clock, and even though we are on a farm, there's not any rooster's cock-a-doodle-dooing because Yasgur's farm is a dairy farm. I go into the cornfield, and when I'm done I walk through to see the field in full daylight. Holy Shit! Last night there were maybe a hundred hippies in front of the stage, but now it's mobbed with several hundred having planted themselves there, while others roam around in all directions across the field.

I head back to Groovy Way to tell Brian and Sam that there are people already showing up and not just a few, but hundreds. I tell them I didn't see any entrance, and that's when it actually dawns on me, there is no entrance, and there are no fences between the stage and us. I'm not sure what that means, but it's Friday the 15th of August, the day the concert begins, and we're in, and that's all that matters.

We have brought mostly canned foods, but thought it wise to eat eggs this morning with cheese and milk, as they will go bad first. We felt pretty good once we ate and walk to fill our half-empty canteens from our watering pipe before we head out to the field. We plan to lay blankets down, so we have our seating for when the concert begins.

I notice Gail a couple of tents away on the other side of the path. She has on tight blue-jean shorts that are ragged at the bottom with a bright pink top. She's with some bearded guy. I guess that's the "we" I didn't ask about last night. I don't remember seeing him at all the night before, but I don't remember anyone except Gail. She sees me, smiles, and gives a nod, then she turns toward the Bearded

One and hands him a canteen. I feel strongly that last night was just a one-time thing, but little did I know what was to come.

I swear when Brian, Sam, and I got to the open field there were now ten times more people than I saw earlier. There must have been thousands; I've never seen so many people in one place, not even in Central Park at a free concert. We walk on to Festival Field to find a place to nest, we figure we would need the restroom and food occasionally, so we plant ourselves right between the stage and the cornfield, which is on the outer edge of The Bowl. We have a slight issue about being under those scaffolds also, just in case they fall over, so we decide we don't want to sit too close.

As the crowd continues to arrive, the hippies just lay their belongings down – blankets, large towels, backpacks, and sleeping bags, anything they brought, like homesteaders making their claim for the land they plan to settle on. We do likewise on this grassy meadow with three blankets we fold in half, one for each of us. We chose this spot because it has a slight incline in our favor to see the stage. Sam found a branch yesterday and attaches some cloth on top like a flag, and now he's sticking it into the ground, so we could use it as a landmark. The open field with all the people will make it near impossible to see our little flag, so I look around to get my bearings. I can't risk not being able to find my way back, so I check out the angle of the stage from the cornfield and decide to use that for my bearings. Now that my blanket is guarding my space, I head out alone to see what is going on. I don't see any fences yet, but if they spring up, my back pocket is holding my ticket for three days of peace and music; at least that's what it said on the posters.

By the way, the Woodstock promoters created the slogan "Three Days of Peace and Music." They were hoping the word, "peace" would help avoid any violence and maybe even appeal to anti-war supporters. The image of the dove perched on the guitar neck is the brainchild of artist Arnold Skolnick, and originally started out as a catbird and a flute. Today, it remains one of the most recognizable iconic images in the world of music.

I head down towards the stage to see how it looks close up, and as I walk, I can see that everyone is happy, and I can move freely through the crowd because this meadow is gigantic. I see lots of guys with long hair down below their shoulders, and some with ponytails halfway down their backs. Others have hair flowing out from under their hats, headbands, and scarfs, and many hippies have beards and mustaches. I see lots of backpacks and babies on backs. Lit joints and wine are being past around nonchalantly.

There's no less than hundreds, but there has to be thousands of concertgoers who have arrived and are already sitting in front, way up to the stage. I'm not that close, but still approaching the stage area. The closer I get the more people I encounter and I finally get to the back of the seated spectators and at this point I can't walk forward any more and just stand there.

We hear the first words spoken over the loud speakers,

> "People in front here, you are too close to the stage. We need room here, and besides, you are too close to see the musicians up here. I'm asking this whole crowd to stand and pick up your stuff. I'm going to start at ten and count downwards and would like you all to take ten giant steps away from the stage. Ten . . . nine . . . eight . . . "

The people all stand up, pick up their things, and start walking towards me. The whole crowd, amazingly, cooperates and when the voice reaches "one," I can see two guys quickly run from the stage area and hammer two posts into the ground and stretch out a rope between the crowd and the stage. This is just one sign of how the hippies of Woodstock are cooperating, and believe me, it's is a sight to behold.

Let me tell you about Chip Monck, the person who has just spoken to the crowd and got us all to move back. Chip Monck brings comfort to the whole atmosphere. His strong voice and fatherly presence emits nothing less than confidence, and he is the major voice throughout the whole concert. He makes numerous announcements and will be introducing the performers; he's the acting emcee.

He got this job by being in the right place at the right time. He's a well-known lighting designer who Woodstock Ventures contracted to set up the stage and the lighting for the concert. It's Friday, and a few hours ago, at 7:00 a.m., when Michael Lang realized he had forgotten something, he walked up to Chip, tapped him on the shoulder and said, "Oh! By the way, we've neglected to hire an emcee, so you're it." Chip had nowhere to go, so he took the job. His first act in this position was to get this crowd to move back from the stage, and he did it masterfully.

There's also an incident in the crowd where someone has clinched fists, and Chip said, "There's not going to be any of that here."

During the whole weekend, he makes us feel safe because he's in control. He gives us pertinent information and warnings. Michael picked the right guy to emcee as far as I'm concerned. By the way, with such little time to set up the stage, the roof isn't strong enough to hold the lighting equipment that was brought, so it went under the stage unused. The only two lights to grace the stage are from the spotlights anchored to the tall scaffolding that Gail and I saw being welded to the high platforms last night.

CHAPTER 5: The Big Announcement

I head away from the stage through the mass of people who are anxiously and yet euphorically looking for spots to plant themselves. I hear another voice over the speakers giving a warning:

> "Please, people in that crane area, please move out, please don't sit near it because when the crane swings, you're gonna get conked on the head, and it's really gonna hurt."

I wouldn't need to be asked twice. Obviously, there is still work that needs to be done because a crane is still needed. It shows just how behind the work is, and without fences to keep the people out, they just keep on coming in.

Once out from the concert bowl, I'm on the accompanying grounds and get a great whiff of marijuana. I can actually see hippies smoking because there is no fear or secrecy here. I particularly see one nonchalant fellow leaning against a tree offering his joint to the newcomers that are arriving. There isn't a better way to feel the peace and love than to share a popular mellowing substance, the drug of choice . . . "Marijuana Exhibit A," as Jerry Garcia would say. So I watch him for a couple of minutes offering his joint to others, some say no, but most take a hit. An old, shaggy-bearded man, walking with a thick branch that he uses as a cane, seems to be looking for the Promised Land. He just might have found it, and even he stops for a moment to take a puff and then continues on his way. I think it might be nice to share a thought with the Joint Man, so I walk over to him.

"Hi," I say. "You sure make a nice welcoming committee."

"What do you mean?"

"You're kind of welcoming the new arrivals by offering them a hit of your weed."

"Oh yeah! Thanks. Would you like one?"

"Well, it does smell sweet . . . sure."

"Don't take too much too fast," he warns.

It has almost no taste at all – very smooth. So smooth that I don't realize how much I am taking in until I start coughing.

"I warned ya, man!"

I try to get out the words "good stuff" between all the coughing, and he hears me.

"Yeah, I know." He says.

"Pretty surreal here, don't you think?" I say, once my coughing ceases.

"Yeah, there are a lot of groovy people here."

"So where do you think they're letting the people in from?" I ask.

"I think everybody's just walking in from everywhere, man, but earlier, there was a fence."

"I'm looking for fences, but I haven't seen any."

"It was way over in that direction," he points, "but it's not up anymore. There weren't any guards, so a couple of guys trying to climb over it, just yanked a section down instead, so a bunch of us just walked right through."

"Really, I got here yesterday with a couple of friends, and we didn't see any fences, so we just parked and set up our tent."

He continues,

"At first I hitched here, but once that car couldn't get any closer I just got out and started walking. I must have left that ride about three miles back and just walked till I got here. Everyone was walking and I'm glad they knocked down that fence. I don't have a ticket, man."

A small cluster of newcomers were upon us, so the Joint Man, did what he does best and offers them a taste of his stash and they stop in their tracks, so I thank him and continue on my way as I hear one of them starting to cough.

I can see friends greeting friends, while others are making friends or at least acquaintances for this wild weekend. People are offering food and drinks to others as the wave of hippies keeps coming. They don't look like campers, just hippies coming to a concert. These are the young kids of today like myself, except I came prepared to camp with my own food and shelter. Most look like they brought only the clothes on their back, although some did have backpacks or small sacks, but nothing close to a three-day supply of anything.

As I look out I can see the rural scenery full of trees in the distance and the grassy part of the land that is accommodating buses, trucks, and trailers. These are the vehicles that are bringing the campers to the outskirts of Yasgur's farm, where camping areas are set up. There are a few campsites closer to all the action, like where we set up, but most are further away. A few of the psychedelic buses also got here early. Let me not mislead you, people are camping everywhere, but the areas set up specifically for camping have the bigger vehicles and larger groups of travelers. The hippies that have come in cars or by foot after abandoning their cars are laying their belongings anywhere, but most are heading towards Festival Field where they will stay and sleep for the duration of the concert.

The road we drove in on has cars parked on either side as far back as I can see. Those cars will remain till the end of the festival, and the pathway between them is entirely crammed with newcomers approaching and passing me. Without skipping a beat, they walk around me and around anybody or anything without much disturbance. Occasional there is a gap in the flow, but otherwise there is a steady stream of travelers walking shoulder to shoulder, three or four people across. There's such an assortment of visitors arriving, but once they reach here, they disperse in all directions throughout the land. I'm just bewildered at the sight.

The people aren't finding any resistance from fences or ticket collectors; no one is directing them to The Bowl or anywhere else – it seems as if no one is in charge. Hippies just pass me smiling and laughing. I can hear their joy in their words, "I think we're here now," We finally made it," and "Which way should we go now?"

I hear the chatter of excitement all around me and I find myself walking next to two girls with backpacks. I over hear one say, "Blossom, I'm thirsty, can we stop and find some water?"

Flower children I assume, wearing flower headbands, not real, plastic and elastic, but they look cute with them on and the one called Blossom has on a long colorful necklace while the other girl has a short one with a peace sign attached. They look very much alike. I start a conversation,

"Hi!"

"Peace!" They greet back.

We all stop walking and I can sense they're tired.

"I'm Glenn."

"I'm Snowflake, and this is my sister, Blossom. Can you please help take this thing off my back?"

"Yeah, sure."

Once off, I ask Blossom if she wants help too.

"God, yes, please." She answers. "Do you know where we can get some water? We just walked here from the town."

"You mean Bethel?"

"Yes!" Snowflake answers.

"That's far. Here, have some of mine," I say, unscrewing the cap.

"You sure? Snowflake asks. "We don't want to take your only water. Where can we get some of our own?"

"Just take a drink," Blossom says, "I'm thirsty."

"There are lines in various places to get water, but please drink as much as you want."

"Really? Well, that's very nice. Thanks," says Snowflake.

She proceeds to drink while Blossom tells me of their adventure.

"The streets in the town were swarming with hippies sleeping everywhere. Traffic was at a standstill with empty cars. We actually abandoned our car on the other side of the town and started walking. In Bethel there were long lines of people sleeping in front of every store, and that was early, 5 a.m. this morning before any places were open. Everyone was hoping to buy food and supplies, but we didn't think we would even get in any store so we kept walking. We past a gas station on this side of town, it had a sign in the window telling everybody they were out of food, but they still had gas, and would open at 7 a.m., and there was a long line from the pump."

"That's crazy." I say.

Snowflake hands the canteen to her sister and says,

"You think that's crazy? When we walked out of town and were halfway here, there were residents trying to sell us bottled water for eight dollars."

"That's not cool, "I say. "You'll find it a lot better here, nearly everyone is sharing, just about anything."

"Are they as gracious as you've been with your water?" Snowflake asks.

"Even more so, I answer. "You can even get high here."

"I don't do that," Blossom says, handing back my canteen.

"You will before you leave here," I assure her.

"Definitely!" Snowflake says emphatically. "That's what I've been telling her. Here Glenn, I have something for you." She slips a beaded bracelet off her wrist and hands it to me.

"That's not necessary."

"Please, you're the nicest person we've met so far."

"That's because you just got here."

"So you better take it before I give it to someone else," she says smiling.

The bracelet is just under an inch wide and is made up of tiny colored beads. The design has two zigzag lines of small black and white beads, like a W running all the way around it. The upper side of the W has the alternating colors of yellow and pink while the under side has alternating colors of red and turquoise. The whole band is elastic, so I just slip it on my wrist.

"She made that herself," Blossom says, proud of her sister.

"Thanks, it's actually very beautiful."

"Do you know where the concert's gonna be?" Snowflake asks.

"Yeah, right down that way," I say, pointing in the direction of The Bowl.

"Thanks."

They head towards Festival Field carry their packs by hand. I call out "Snowflake," and when she turns around I hold up my hand, shaking my wrist with the bracelet on it, "Thanks," and she smiles back holds up a peace sign and shouts back, "Peace."

It has been recorded, wherever they record such things that 90 % of the attendees smoked marijuana. Acid and other psychedelics were used and there was one reported death from a heroin overdose and an estimated 400 participants treated for bad acid trips. I'm pretty sure Blossom will get high.

I'm heading to the wooded area and when I reach it there are hippies congregating like friends on a busy little street corner in the Bronx. They're lingering, talking, and smoking. As I move through the cluster I see at the edge of the woods some shops set up. Hippies have opened up a smoke shop by placing a long table as a counter in front of themselves. They display pipes, papers, and other drug related paraphernalia, but I'm not sure this little stand has permission to be here. The concession stands that are allowed are near the "Food for Love" area.

Another stand has a friendly couple selling tie-dye square pieces of material like scarfs or wall hangings in 3' by 3' sections. Some of those psychedelic tapestries are draped over the counter, while other colorful pieces hang from a clothesline attached to trees on either side of their stand. Those beautiful multicolored images hanging over their heads are attracting hippies like moths to a light.

Followers of Che Guevara found a spot to set up camp, as well, and hang a banner above their heads between two trees, that reads, "A TRUE REVOLUTIONARY is guided by great feelings of love. Che."

Amateur musicians are sitting and strumming on their guitars, while others just walk by with their guitars strapped over their shoulders looking for their own little place to play. A family is setting up camp in front of their psychedelic bus, while their naked children play, and when I say family I mean a small communal group who traveled here together. I see others walking around carrying flowers, food, drinks, and blankets, but I didn't expect to see joints being smoked in the open, while passing within 20 feet of a policeman.

There's a guy wearing a worn cowboy hat pulled down right above his eyes and has on a white jump suit from head to toe. There is a red, white, and blue patch on his arm. He's using a walking stick as he's humming into his a kazoo.

A bus is moving slowly with hippies standing on the hood, on the bumpers, and on the roof. They didn't just get here though; no vehicles can, but they obviously chose to move it from where it was. It went from blocking the pathway over to where it's now out of the way.

I didn't expect to see kids either, but they're here, screaming and laughing, while being entertained by riding in a cart being pulled by a small tractor. It's obvious to me this weekend is gonna be much more than just a concert and even more than just a festival.

Here are girls wearing jean shorts with swimsuit tops, actually no, they're bras. Is there really a difference though? Underwear is sexier. Now I'm thinking about Gail, and she didn't even have on a bra. A few nuns are walking by and even though I'm Jewish, I still feel guilty when nuns are involved. It's funny how my thoughts went to Gail and not Sharon back at camp. I dated Sharon most of the summer. She was interesting and we hung out every night, she was my summer fling, but she chose not to come with me, it would have been really nice. I have to stop thinking of her. I wonder where Gail is now.

I'm passing a parked bus that has an American flag on it and another flag that says, "Even God loves America." Flower children are dancing to the music coming out from the bus windows. Some are just waving their arms in the air or jerking their bodies to the beat. Some are lying on blankets swaying their heads. Even I'm walking with rhythm in my steps as I pass through this gathering. It's almost noon, and the whole place is alive.

As I continue walking, I see a group of women performing silently, wearing rope belts around their waists with a square patch in back covering their ass and a square patch in front covering their . . . fronts, just like Indians I've seen in Westerns. The men are bare-chested, wearing beads, and the girls have flowers in their hair. It's just so wonderful being here with all the free-spirit energy. Everyone is happy, and there's music in the air. As the music from the bus fades, I hear the sounds of a flute and bongos like they played last night.

I'm standing watching a policeman talking with a woman as hippies are walking by smoking joints. The officer looks up for a second, sniffing the air and goes back to his conversation. I say out loud, but to myself, "This is like the lions lying down with the lambs." A hippie standing next to me is holding a rope tied to his pet sheep and says, "That's from the Bible, my brother, it's Isaiah 11:6, only it talks about wolves lying with lambs." He's carrying a sign that says, "Killing animals creates killing man," and I'm thinking, "Killing that sheep would create a great lamb chop," but I better not convey my thoughts to him. As long as I'm on the subject of animals, I might add that there are many dogs roaming around, none on leashes, but they all seem friendly enough.

I turn and spot a topless woman with a body painting of a peace sign around her left breast, while she's holding her naked child in front of her other one. I notice everywhere clothes made with the American flag. The image or colors are on shirts, pants, and hats, and even flags are being used as capes. The people here are not only peaceful, but it appears to me that they're very patriotic. I guess we all know there is no better place on Earth than America.

I'm getting close to the arena again and decide to take another look, and I can see that it's filling up. The crowds of settlers have planted themselves in unrelated areas across the field, like when you're working on a jigsaw puzzle, after you have the outside together you start to piece different groups on the inside until they connect to each other. Now those little groups are starting to connect making for one very large blanket of people sprawled across this wide-open space.

I can see that love isn't only in the air, but also on the ground. A woman is on top of a guy, no shirts on either of them, embracing and kissing. A man is on top of a woman grinding in public, many holding hands, some rubbing or squeezing every part of their companion's body. It's a "festival on a blanket." Others around don't seem to care, but you won't catch me doing that.

I hear feedback screeching over the speakers, and now a man's voice coming through loud and clear. It's John Morris, Head of Production at Woodstock, and he's making an announcement:

> "This is one thing that I was going to wait awhile before we talked about, but maybe we'll talk about it now, so you can think about it because you all, we all, have to make some kind of plan for ourselves. It's a free concert from now on. That doesn't mean that anything goes though. What that means is we are going to put the music up here for free. What that means is the people, who put the backing for this thing, the money, are going to take a bath, a big bath. That's not hype, that's the truth, and they're going to get hurt. What it means is, to these people, is that your welfare and the music is a hell of a lot more important than a dollar."

There are cheers from the audience, especially when he said, "free concert," but it's also nice to know they have our backs since our welfare may very well be on the line, and we can count on them. I look far past the crowd on the field, and I see there's still more hippies approaching from the other side. There's a non-stop flow of human beings coming here today, and I'm sure no one is leaving; for today, the next three days, and for now and forever, this is the place known as Woodstock.

CHAPTER 6: The Bridge

I see a group of hippies in a circle passing some wine, and there's an empty space on the blanket, and one of them invites me to join them. I'm a little thirsty for something other than water so I sit down. They're very hospitable. Three of the guys came together and abandoned their car in the middle of the night. They had met these three girls during their hike here, and now they're hanging out together. They told me that by daybreak, they arrived here surrounded by about fifty or sixty other hippies that also abandoned their cars. All seem to have the same story this Friday morning. I'm so glad we got here Thursday.

As I got up to leave, I hear the voice, once again, of John Morris coming over the speakers,

> "How is it out there?" A roar from the crowd follows. "We apologize for the noise of the 'choppity, choppity,' but it seems like there are a few cars blocking the road, so we're flying everybody in. I almost made the worst pun in the world about 'high musicians," but let's skip that."

I leave The Bowl and find myself at another section in front of a wooded area. As I shuffle through a swarm of newcomers, a lit joint suddenly appears in front of my face, offered to me by none other than Brian. Sam is with him, and the three of us are feeling pretty good. We notice a bridge leading through the woods and decide to take it, figuring it's not only a shortcut back to our campsite, but also a great way to stay out of the sun, which is starting to feel hot. So we step up onto the bridge and proceed to walk into the woods while sharing the joint.

It's definitely gets cooler once we step under the tall trees, which might seem even taller than they really are because we're stoned. There are rails on both sides of the bridge; so a little way in, we lean on the rails facing each other to chat as we finish the joint. Sam holds the roach (what's left of the joint) as we have a small debate whether it's biodegradable or not. We can't decide, and Sam refuses to throw it into the woods, so he eats it.

"I'm so glad we got here yesterday," I say.

Both of them agree.

"By the way," Brian says, "I went back to the car to make sure it's still there. It is."

"We are lucky to have parked so close," Sam adds.

"Most everyone that arrived today," I say, "had abandoned their cars. People just want to get here no matter how far it is or how long it takes. I think we can all agree this place is something special."

"Nice bracelet," Brian says, "where'd you get it?"

"It was given to me."

"It looks like a girl's," Sam blurts out, and starts laughing.

"Actually it is," I say. "I met two girls that were thirsty and they told me that some residents in town were trying to rip them off by charging eight bucks for a bottles of water. They didn't buy any and they were thirsty, so I let them have some of my water, and one of them gave me this bracelet in return. Her name was Snowflake."

"Really? Snowflake? Sam mocks. Is that her real name?"

"Yeah, she's a flower child, and you know how that goes, Starlight, Butterfly . . . "

"Sugar free." Sam jokes.

"Her sister was Blossom," I threw in.

"Blossom?" Brian says, and starts giggling.

"Alright, what have you guys been up too?" I ask, wanting to change the subject.

"Well, we went up to the 'Food for Love' area," Brian says, "and there were very long lines. A few of the stands were already closed because they ran out of food and they don't expect to reopen. There's no way to get food into this place except by foot."

"Or helicopter," Sam adds.

I add my own two cents, "I can't believe how many out-of-towners came so unprepared."

Brian agrees and says, "We're lucky we have that water pipeline, we already saw a long line at the water spigots. They have set them up in rows, so attendees can wash off their feet and bodies. There are also water fountains for drinking. There are a lot of thirsty people there, and they're all waiting in line very patiently."

"In fact," Sam says, "it's a great way to meet people.

"I haven't had any problem with that. Is there any crowd at our water supply?" I inquire.

"No, not there," Brian says, and then whispers, "It's an unknown spot."

Then precisely at the same time we each unscrew the caps to our canteens, lift each in the air and tap all three together.

"Peace! Love! Rock & Roll!" we say in unison. Then we all take a swig of water, swallow and start laughing as we move on.

The trail takes a curve and when we look back the view of the entrance is block by trees. There were some hippies on the bridge in front of us, but they're gone now, since we stopped. We feel like we're in the middle of the woods, far from the maddening crowd, but safe on the little wooden bridge.

"We ran into Denise," Sam says.

"Oh yeah! Is she with anybody?"

"Yeah! She's with two girlfriends, but we didn't know either one of them. She asked if they could sit with us tomorrow, for a while. Brian told them it was fine and we're gonna meet them at the cornfield in the morning."

"Are they like her?"

"What do you mean? Brian asks.

"Well, Denise can be a little snobbish, you know. Are they like that?"

"We didn't really talk with them," Brian says, "but they were dressed like her, though. What do you think, Sam?

They're her friends." Sam answers. "Of course they're like her."

"Maybe her friends are different," I say.

"Yeah!" Sam says. "Like we're different from each other,

right. Look at us."

We start laughing.

"You're right, I withdraw the question."

There is another slight curve on our path, and a clearing through the trees shows light at the end of the bridge. There are plenty of people passing at the end, so onward we go. We made up our minds that when we get back to the campsite we're gonna get some wine and cheese, fill our canteens, and venture out to our three blankets that lay side, by side, by side, somewhere in the wide-open space of Festival Field with a little flag signaling for us to come home.

We reach the end of the bridge and take a step down to get back onto solid ground. I swear we don't walk ten steps when we see another bridge in front of us going into the woods.

"Hey, guys!" I say. "That's not another bridge. It's the same bridge we just took into the woods. It curves around and made a complete circle."

"Are you sure?" Sam asks.

"Yeah! We took the furthest route to get nowhere. See! We are in the same place that you guys met me."

We really start laughing now and almost can't stop, but we do.

"I think I'm gonna skip the wine," I say, "and head down to the lake I saw from the hill yesterday."

"Oh!" Brian says. "We learned it's not a lake, it's a pond. Filippini Pond to be exact, but we're still gonna go back to the campsite and then head out to the field."

"That's a great idea," Sam agrees. "I have to get some toilet paper and check out the cornfield."

"I'll meet you back at the blankets before the concert begins," I assure them. Then I see a couple that look stoned getting on the bridge, but I don't say a word.

CHAPTER 7: Filippini Pond

I can see the stage towards my right as I head down to Filippini Pond, and as I'm en route, there's a couple of girls, youngsters, blowing bubbles into the air. I try to avoid the bubbles and step to my left and dart to my right, any movement to successfully slip between the bubbles, so I won't be hit. The little girls start blowing more and more bubbles as they giggle and I eventually can't dodge them all and fall to the ground when I'm finally hit. The girls continue giggling as I get up and continue on my way. Then I pass a long line that I think is for water like Sam had mentioned, but this line is for the telephone. I can hear one caller, "I'm telling you, they're not taking tickets. You can get in free. Really!"

I think to myself, "Yeah, you can get in for free, you just can't get here."

There isn't anyone I want to call, and even if there was, I don't have change for the phone. I continue strolling to the far end of Mr. Yasgur's farm to where the land meets the water and the water reaches the sky or at least the other side of the pond.

As I continue to walk, I observe a Hare Krishna, and even though everyone is so nice to each other offering food and water or whatever, this one Krishna guy is grubbing money. It seems to me money is the last thing you need here unless you want to use the phone, but here he is, this one member with what appears to be an upside down tambourine scrounging for money. He's in some orange garb, wears glasses, and is bald. What can you do? What's funny is not two minutes later I'm passing a Rasta man with his head full of hair, just the opposite of Mr. Krishna and too laid back to ask for anything. In fact, with his dreadlocks stuffed into his red, yellow, and green knit hat, he looks at me and offers me a taste of his ganja. How could I say no to that smiling face with his bright white teeth shining at me?

I'm flying pretty high when I finally reach the water, and I'm in for an awesome sight. I don't really think "awesome," probably more like "groovy" or maybe "far out." I'm even more excited now than when I saw girls in their bras because these girls are naked in the water. Boys and girls are skinny-dipping, and I've been walking with the sun beating down on me, hoping to be able to go into the water to cool off. Skinny-dipping never entered my mind, but I'm sure gonna join in.

First I take off my shirt knocking off my bandana, but I put it back on, then my shoes and socks. I take off the colorful bracelet that had been given to me and stuff it into the pocket of my pants and continue to take them off, and my underwear, which seems a little tight anyway, and lay them all folded with my canteen on top. Now I feel good, with nothing on, but my red bandana.

As I walk into the water, I can see some women with their dark triangular patches below their waists since the water is only up to our knees. Then, I see one woman that looks shaved, but it's only because she's a blonde. I catch up with them and as the water gets higher, I start to realize that I better get into even deeper water quickly, because it's becoming very obvious to me that I'm becoming very obvious to them. As we all get further in, the dark triangles disappear below the surface, but I'm not as lucky as they are since my object is floating near the surface, raising its head up every now and then like the Loch Ness monster. It doesn't help that I'm still looking at the women and notice that some are big, some small and some perky. I don't know if I mention this, but I'm only 19, and I've never been around anything like this. Even though I'm in up to my waist, I can feel my organ playing a tune. When I look down, it's under the water, but too close to the surface for it to be hidden. I look away from the women, which is a good thing because I'm becoming a little self-conscious about staring, I mean looking, at them. I know I'm naked while skinny-dipping, but being excited is a little embarrassing for me.

A couple walks close to me, and I force myself not to stare at the female's perky little breasts by turning my head away. I swear I only look for a hundredth of a second, maybe a tenth. She passes even closer to me than the guy does, and then I feel her hand grip me. She gives it a tight squeeze and a jerk and lets go. I'm shocked, but it's so quick I keep looking away like it's an accident. Then I hear her whisper, "Oh! I'm sorry, did I startle you?" I know that voice – that's Gail.

At this point, she's already past me and I look towards her, she's looking back and winks. I swallow hard, go down in the water up to my neck, and watch her exit the pond. She has on pink panties, which goes with the pink blouse I saw her in this morning. I would rather watch her behind than some of the bare ass women in the water. I can see her young shapely body and what appears to be a birthmark right under her left cheek. Seeing that didn't help my situation under the water, especially after the grab, but I continue watching her until she's out of the water and out of sight.

Once she disappears, I stand up and turn around, and there in front of me is a woman with large sagging breasts. I quickly raise my head up, but it's too late. I see them, huge and dangling downward with stretch marks all over. I think the pond is only up to her waist, but her nipples hang down and can still reach the water. I thought, "What could be worse?" Then, I notice she's pregnant. A pregnant woman is a beautiful sight, I mean usually a beautiful sight when she's in clothes, which is the only way I've ever seen them until now. One thing for sure is now I can leave the pond, and my penis will draw absolutely no attention since it's no longer at attention.

I leave the water and go to the shore to get dressed and get out of here. I put my clothes back on, grab my canteen, but decide to drop my underwear in the first trash receptacle I can find. I simply don't want to wear them anymore. As I walk away from the pond

I still have the opportunity to see naked girls dash past me, but I don't dare turn around. I just enjoy the frontal exposure rather than turning to see their rear ends for fear of accidentally seeing Godzilla again.

Some very tall guy asks me how the water is.

"It's not to cold," I answer, "but only waist deep for me, so you better go in on your knees."

I don't think he got the joke.

Even though I'm away from the pond, there are still some exposed breast to be seen bouncing around periodically. I really try not to be caught staring, and I found the easiest way to do that is to simply not stare. I've learned a lesson, and I have a motto now, "If you see one . . . you've seen them both."

CHAPTER 8: The Medical Tent

I leave the pond and now see the tops of the cranes, and I decide to head towards them because that's the way to The Bowl. There's a helicopter flying right over my head, and it's turning in the direction of the highway. I approach a large pink and white tent and walk around to the front of it. On the side of the opening is a sign that reads Medical Tent. There's quite a commotion going on inside where I see a guy freakin' out.

I step into the tent, and this guy in a T-shirt is speaking loud and incoherently, more like part of words than full words. He began hitting himself with one hand like a slap to his cheek, but not real hard, then his hand slides down his neck, while his other hand just sways back and forth uncontrollably. Then, he starts laughing, loud and swaying his body, and I'm close enough to see his eyes roll back into his head showing just the whites, I think he's about to pass out, but they come back.

A huge guy in a teal medics uniform with an identification tag that has the name Larry K, is standing ready to grab him if he gets dangerous, but instead the guy starts whimpering and crosses his hands at his wrists like he's in handcuffs and then pulls his hands up to his chest. "Am I dying?" he asks. Those are the first words I can understand. "Where am I? Am I dying?" His legs seem weak and give out. Larry grabs his arm helping him drop slowly to the ground, and lets him go. He's rolling back and forth laughing, but no sooner he begins crying again.

"Where am I? Am I dying?" he says, spitting his words out and his eyes are very glossy. Larry asks a smaller guy in a white outfit if he should hold him down. "No," the guy answers. "Don't hold him down, just pick him up and hold him steady."

Wait a minute that guy looks familiar. I know him. He's the guy I saw playing his kazoo earlier. I recognize him because he's still in his white jumpsuit, and holding his worn hat. I thought he was a doctor, he doesn't seem to be, but he's helping.

Larry gets him up on his feet and holds him in place while the Kazoo Guy starts trying to communicate with him. Quickly asking, "What's your name? What is your name?"

This guy has no idea what is happening to him and just sort of moans. Larry stands by his side not letting go. "This is Larry," Kazoo Guy says. "Who are you? Can you tell Larry who you are? He's gonna help you."

It doesn't seem like this guy is responding, but then all of a sudden he says, "Bob, I think I'm Bob." Kazoo Guy looks at what appears to be a driver's license. "Good Bob, you are Bob, I see it here. Good, you know you're Bob." Bob is bobbing his head affirmatively, and seems to understanding.

Kazoo guy's talking slowly and clearly.

"Okay, Bob, you've taken something bad, but it won't hurt you. You're not gonna die. You just need it to wear off. You just took some bad acid. Do you know what I'm saying, Bob? You're gonna be alright."

Bob's not moving his hands around anymore and not making any sounds. He's swaying very slightly, trying to balance himself as Larry holds him. He seems somewhat lethargic, but calm, and somewhat responsive.

"You're on a bad trip. You're not gonna die. You're with friends and you're in our clinic. You will come down soon and everything will be normal, Bob. Can you nod your head so we know you understand."

He nods slowly.

"Good, Bob, very good. You're with good people, who will take good care of you until you come down."

This guy is really good, I think to myself. He calmed Bob down to at least the point where he seems emotionally stable and he has stopped him from hitting himself physically. Bob responds enough that the Kazoo Guy motions to Larry, and tells Bob, "Larry's gonna take you to a cot in the other tent for you to rest. You won't be the only one there, but there are medical people to help you till you come down. Okay? You'll come out of it soon enough. I promise."

I hope Bob trusts him because I'm convinced he wouldn't have promised, if it weren't true.

With that crisis over, it's still chaotic because many participants are coming in with bloody feet from walking around barefoot; some need medicine for their headache, stomachache or a splint for a broken bone. Another guy arrives with his friend and informs them about some brown acid that his friend has taken. It's a little too chaotic for me, but after all, it's an infirmary. Since I don't need help and don't want to be in the way, I continue heading to the field to meet my friends.

Along the way I pass a chain link fence surrounding a large grass meadow, which leads behind the stage. I'm walking along the fence and see the heliport. It's the only way the musicians can get in and out of here. I can also see the Performers Pavilion where the acts hang out and the entrance to the bridge. That bridge was especially constructed to go over that paved road. There's security all around this area, and after talking with one of the security guards I learn that Woodstock Ventures had to pay for a permit to build that bridge over that little paved road, which is actually West Shore Road. That's the road we took to get here, but turned off it to get to our campsite.

From here, I can see the staff and performers sitting at tables eating and drinking. I think I see Jack Casady from the Jefferson Airplane; he's always wearing a bandana like me, and next to him is his fellow band mate Jorma on a mini motorcycle. That's a great way to get around this area. I'm not 100 percent sure, but I think I see Jerry Garcia from The Grateful Dead. I swear it looks like him rolling a joint. Wow! It would be far out to get high with him.

"JERRY! JERRY!"

Some guy next to me starts yelling. He thinks its Jerry Garcia too. Holy Shit! He looks this way and it's . . . it is Jerry Garcia. The yelling got his attention. Jerry's standing up and he's walking this way.

"HEY JERRY! JERRY!" Again this guy yells.

He's right upon us on the other side of the fence. His hair and his beard seem like a continuous woolly, shaggy, furry mane of a lion, with hair shooting across his upper lip hiding his mouth completely. His glasses have perfectly round frames with orange-tint lenses, and here's wearing a plain blue T-shirt.

"Hey, how you doing guys?" Jerry asks.

The guy next to me asks, "When are you gonna play, man?"

"Tomorrow evening if all goes well."

He lights up the joint, and I can see more distinctly where his mouth is. He turns his head away from us to blow the smoke out. The guy asks, "What are you gonna play?"

"Don't know yet."

I just have to butt in, "Have you ever seen a crowd like this, Jerry?"

I think I see a smile on his face, but who can tell?

> "Has anyone ever seen a crowd like this? He answers. It's cool, man."

He turns the joint around and hands it to me through one of the links of the fence. I take a hit and nod as if asking for permission to hand it off to the guy next to me. "Sure," he says, and nods his approval.

Then he says, "We flew in earlier this morning and saw all the traffic backed up wondering how far we'd have to go to get here. It was a never-ending freeway of cars. This huge gathering is almost biblical, man. Where did all those people even come from? I've never seen so many people in my life."

> "It's really unbelievable," I respond, "and they can only get here by foot. Oh! And there's probably more coming because it's a free concert now."

Jerry acknowledges he knows that.

> "Once that was announced," I say, "people were calling friends, but I don't know how close people can really get, probably not close enough to even walk here."

The guy hands Jerry back the joint, and a crowd is starting to form around us. I can hear, "Hey man," "Jerry," "Wow!"

> "Stay cool, guys," he says, as he turns and walks away.

> "You too, Jerry, thanks," I say.

That's another far out thing that's happened to me – first Gail, then skinny-dipping and now Jerry Garcia. Who knew this could get better.

By the way it may be a free concert for the other concertgoers, but not for me. Remember, I had already purchased my ticket and it definitely isn't free for promoters John Roberts and Joel Rosenman, who still have to pay the performers. In Jerry Garcia's case, his band was paid $2,500, which today is like $16,000. Make note though, you can't get the Grateful Dead today for $16,000, and definitely not with Jerry Garcia, who died in 1995 from a heart attack while in a rehabilitation clinic.

As I approach Festival Field, it's late afternoon, and it amazes me to see The Bowl completely full from the stage to the brim. I have to travel through three quarters of this field to get back to my little blanket and with this crowd I have no idea if it's possible. I guess I could walk on the outside of this arena and come down through the cornfield, but what the hell; I'll give it a try from here.

As I venture through The Bowl, I find pathways through or around groups of spectators. It's a challenge, and makes the walk slow. I manage to move freely through the field, but at times my feet don't seem to be moving at all. There are times when I purposely stop for the occasional joint that I help pass from one blanket to another or the bottle of wine I help open for someone. I do take a drink because the sun is beating down on me.

It's actually a challenge making my way across this landscape of free-spirited people. I'm following others, and I'm being followed like ants on their way to a picnic. There's another group of ants marching in the opposite direction to some other picnic. I see lots of joints as I walk and lovers kissing, hugging, and feeling each other up, just shy of doing more. Radios are playing and hippies are swaying, while others stare at the stage as if in a trance, and even others lay on their blankets asleep.

Chip's strong radio voice fills the air once again,

> "John, please meet Sally at the southwest gate. She needs her medication."

I overhear someone as I pass say, "That means Sally wants to get high, and John has her stuff." I think to myself, "Really? That's what it means? That's cool."

As I proceed on my course to my friends, Chip continues,

> "Ellen Savage, please call your father at the Motel Glory in Woodridge. Ellen Savage, please call your father at the Motel Glory in Woodridge."

I can't imagine what that message is code for; maybe Ellen's father just wants her to call the motel.

I start to laugh to myself about the little flag that sits upon a branch somewhere to guide me to my blanket. Even if I have a telescope, I'm sure I couldn't find it. Everyone's sitting patiently for the concert to begin. Just being here among all these hippies, sharing food, drinks, drugs, and conversation is so far-out I don't really care when it starts.

As I walk through the crowd it seems like my progress is slower than I anticipated. Everyone is polite and excuses the stepping on their blankets, but I'm not sure each step takes me closer to me destination. It doesn't feel like it until I look at the stage and see that I've come further along or as I look back and see the distance from where I started, is now further away, so I guess I am making progress.

A plane is crossing the sky and seems to be moving very fast. That's unusual, I think to myself, but maybe it just seems that way because I'm stoned. I don't remember seeing planes moving so quickly though, but what do I know? Suddenly, there is a loud BOOM! It seems to silence the crowd for a whole tenth of a second before the crowd roars with cheers. I pass a group talking about it and learn it's a sonic boom, which is caused by an object traveling through the air faster than the speed of sound. Really?

The plane moves faster than the speed of sound? Can that really happen? Yes, it can I'm told. The plane sort of pushes the sound waves all together until they pile up on each other and explode, causing the loud boom we just heard. Obviously it's done for us down here on earth at Woodstock.

I look toward the stage and toward the cornfield, working my way in between to where I feel my friends should be. Smiles accompany me the whole way, and I feel we all know we're at something special, but I hope everyone understands like I do that we're making it special. It's our being peaceful, friendly, sharing, smiling, and any other positive adjective that one wishes to use that is making this work. This is the only time that I can ever remember that we all look different, but we're all the same. As I continue walking through the heat, there's a blurry sense of people and faces, which all blend together as I tiptoe at times through the crowd.

I see someone waving, but can't make out whom it is. I don't believe it's someone from my blanket since I know that's further away and they're probably waving to someone behind me anyway. As I get closer I can see her face clearer, she's waving and smiling at me. It's Sharon. What the hell is she doing here? My first and only reaction is to look away as if I don't see her and I continue on my way. I do manage to move on without looking back and as I turn my head to my right, I can see the little cloth hanging down from the stick that proclaims this area to be my turf, and there is Brian and Sam. They brought the bread, the cheese, and the wine.

I'm not as far from Sharon as I would like to be, but I'll just forget she's there, after all, she's not interested in me any more and I've been doing fine without her and yet I still wonder what she's doing here. She was smiling, but with the entire place high on weed, who wouldn't be? Still, she was smiling and waving at me. What gives?

I join Brian and Sam telling them about going down to the pond and about smoking with Jerry Garcia, even though it was only one hit.

They told me they saw writing on a tent, "This is Pure Insanity." We all agree with that message. Then Sam told me he heard a young man was killed while in a pasture asleep in his sleeping bag. He had been run over by a tractor. That's one of the most terrible things I'd ever heard, and they haven't found who was driving. That's the second casualty. I already told you there was a hippie that died from a heroin overdose, what I didn't mention was that he was a Marine who survived a tour of duty in Vietnam. The third and last death at Woodstock was a person who died of a ruptured appendix and just couldn't get the proper help here.

CHAPTER 9: The Concert Begins

The concert was supposed to start at 2:00 p.m., and it's now almost 5:00 p.m. I look over the crowd and notice for the first time that there are people clinging to the scaffolding that looks down onto the stage. Most are sitting halfway up, but some venture even higher. It doesn't look very comfortable to be sitting up on those rails, but I think it's worse for the ones standing up because they're probably holding on for dear life. They all seem like monkeys staring down towards the stage, and the monkeys below are hoping none will fall.

Brian lights one up, and as we pass it around, we see some commotion on the stage and hope the wait is over. I have enjoyed the day, and I'm waiting patiently for the musicians to take me into the night. As I look back at the scaffolding, it appears to be a giant spider web that has caught these huge flies. I can see arms and legs moving, but it looks like their bodies are stuck.

I stand up and gaze out at the crowd that's been filling up this field all day. I strategically traveled through it to get to my blanket and now I slowly start turning around in my spot and as I do I find myself in the middle of this giant jigsaw puzzle of people. The puzzle looks complete and there's a slight movement across the whole field, and the colors are as numerous as they are different. The lawn is completely covered, not one blade of grass can be seen.

How did I maneuver over this field completely saturated with people in order to get to my friends? Maybe I just took it slow and easy, maybe I was lucky, but I think it's because of the inner workings of the human soul in this Shangri-la. Neighbors are compassionate allowing passage through their kingdom and transcending around their paradise guiding me past their wonderland to my Eden. Damn! Gail's right I talk weird when I'm stoned.

The group Sweetwater is supposed to start the musical portion of the Woodstock Festival because their keyboard player is in the Air Force Reserves and is to report to Uncle Sam this weekend, so they requested early stage time, but they haven't arrived yet because of the traffic jam. Richie Havens was one of the first flown in and is to play this first night, so Michael Lang tells him, "We need something to happen or it's gonna get really crazy out here." So Michael asks him to take the stage. Richie is reluctant to be the first performer of the show, but after a little coaxing, he agrees.

Chip announces the first performer and the concert begins,

> "What better way to start, Ladies and Gentlemen, one of the most beautiful men in the whole world, let's welcome, Mr. Richie Havens!"

Richie comes out to the waiting crowd and after tuning up his guitar he begins with "Handsome Johnny." He's known as a singer-songwriter who plays folk, soul, and blues and also does cover songs. Today he's supposed to play four songs for about 20 minutes, but every time he leaves center stage, he's persuaded to come back and do another set. He goes back six times and plays everything he knows, ending with "Freedom (Motherless Child)," which he improvises. He leaves center stage this time strumming and sweating until he could strum no more, but it's this performance that skyrockets him to a new level of fame. He died in 2013, and, on the anniversary of Woodstock, his ashes were scattered over this field.

The next performer on stage is Satchidananda Saraswati, I'm not sure I would call him a performer, but I'm sure that I can not pronounce his name. He's the Swami and the opening speaker at

Woodstock, and it turns out he's a guru by trade and a philosopher of yoga. It must surely be the weed, but he seems to me to be a funny guy. I'm on my blanket thinking he's a comedian.

> "My Beloved Brothers and Sisters, music is sound, does that sound good? It sounds good to me. America makes some good music. I mentioned this to a Ghandi, there are so many Ghandis, but one is the grandson of Mahatma Gandhi. That is his name, Grandson of Mahatma Gandhi."

What a namedropper, I think to myself.

> "And Grandson of Mahatma Gandhi asked me, 'What's going on in America?' I answer him, I think it's a party, I think?"

> "I told him of a group called 'Fight for Peace.' I don't understand, you fight, you have peace, but if you have peace then who is doing the fighting? A monastery wants me to talk under the heading of 'East and West — One Heart,' but am I from the East or the West? I heard the West is the best. Now, I want all of you out there to chant. I will start, and then, you join in. Hari OM, Hari OM, Hurry, Hurry, Hurry, let's go hOMe."

Then he sings,

> "Rama, Rama, Rama, Rana, Rana. Ran, a Ran a hOMe!" as he leaves the stage.

Now that I know where Sharon's sitting I can't help but glance that way once in a while. I'm far enough away to forget she's here, but close enough and willing to occasionally look her way, and I can see Ken is with her. I can't help thinking what did I do wrong?

Sweetwater finally make it and are coming on next. It's close to 7:30 p.m. now, and the sun is still in the sky. The three of us are very happy where we have planted ourselves to see and hear the performers. If the stage is at 12 o'clock, simply put, our location is at 5 o'clock, halfway between the stage and the outer rim of the field. We are just a dot on this field of dreams and much less active at this hour than we were during the day. Everyone is winding down, but we all get excited as each new act hits the stage. A voice comes on the speakers with an announcement,

"Now, let's face the situation. We've had thousands and thousands of people come here today. Many, many more than we knew or even dreamt could be possible. We are going to need everyone to help each other to work this out because we are taxing the systems that we set up. We're going to be bringing food in, but the one major thing you have to remember tonight when you go back up to the woods to go to sleep or if you stay here, is that the man next to you is your brother, and you damn well better treat each other that way because if you don't, we blow the whole thing."

With that being said, the next the next announcement was simply,

"Ladies and Gentlemen, Sweetwater!"

Sweetwater is the first actual group to perform at Woodstock. Nancy Nevins is the lead singer and has a strong voice that reminds me of Grace Slick. The group performs for about 40 minutes, and her singing is great, but they take too long between songs.

If you haven't heard of Nancy I'm not surprised. Her singing career was cut short four months after Woodstock when she was in a terrible, almost fatal automobile accident. She was in a coma, but luckily she came out of it. Her vocal cords, however, were damaged and she couldn't continue her singing career to the success she was heading for.

The Friday night schedule of Woodstock is billed as the night of folk music. Of course, I already told you that a Swami was here, and later on Ravi Shankar will be playing a few of his greatest hits. I'm not sure how they made it into this category, except that the Swami didn't perform, but talked; The only reason I can think of that Ravi is in this category is that maybe, just maybe, in his country, his music is their folk music.

Next up is 20-year-old Bert Sommer. He has a young boyish face that is almost hidden by his huge Afro-style hair. He's a folksinger whose act is made up of a three-piece ensemble. His rendition of Simon & Garfunkel's "America" is unbelievable; not only is it a highlight of his musical set, but indeed of the whole night. It looks like he's getting a standing ovation, but I'm too high to stand. He has a great sense of humor because back stage, its been reported, he said, "Yeah, I got a standing ovation, they all got up to go to the bathroom."

Even though he had been in the original cast of "*Hair*" and is a promising young artist, the reason he's scheduled to perform at Woodstock is because Artie Kornfeld, one of the promoters, is his agent and feels like this is a great platform to boost his career. Bert later wrote, "We're All Playing in The Same Band," which was a song about Woodstock.

Another full fledge folksinger is coming up next – Tim Hardin. He was originally put on the list to play earlier, but the effect of drugs stopped him from performing until now, after dark. It's not until around 9:00 p.m., that he comes down from the effects of heroin. This night, with a couple of spotlights on him, he does a short set just over 30 minutes, but for me and 499,999 others he does manage to play his classic song, "If I Were a Carpenter." It starts to rain lightly right after his set.

Many artists cover his songs and Bob Dylan calls him "the greatest songwriter alive." A heroin overdose took his life in late 1980.

As the rain starts to fall, Brian, Sam, and myself make the decision to stay on the field and hear more music, rather than go back to our campsite. We aren't gonna let a little rain stop us from hearing groups, especially after waiting a day and a half. It's not raining very heavy, so we just cover ourselves up with plastic sheets that were handed out earlier. We didn't think to take precautions for the possibility of rain when we packed.

This might be a good time to mention some of the folk artists who declined invitations to be here. Bob Dylan was never a serious candidate for coming to the festival. He wasn't happy that hippies were coming so close to the area he lived. Joni Mitchell was invited to perform, but her manager thought it would be more important for her to be on *The Dick Cavett Show*. She has heard all the news reports, as well as hearing all about the weekend from her boyfriend, Graham Nash, when he gets home. Not being here inspires her to write her iconic song, "Woodstock," that has sort of a haunting arrangement when she sings it, but is rearranged as a hard rock song by Crosby, Stills, Nash and Young. It has not only becomes a huge hit for them, but it has become a hippie anthem for our generation.

Now the three of us are safely under cover, we wait patiently for the next group, and it's very fair to say that the time between groups is very short once the concert gets underway. Some of the artists refuse to play in the rain even though they're scheduled, but the rain doesn't bother Ravi Shankar, who appears next. He had appeared at the Monterey Pop Festival sharing his Indian music with the Western world, so the promoters thought he would make a very special addition to the Woodstock Festival. It's about 10:00 p.m., and the rain is starting to come down much harder.

Ravi Shankar's music is far from the music of our Western culture, so we're supposed to open ourselves up to the rhythms and the melodies of his traditional Indian music. Whatever, Ravi, just play your sitar, it's raining and we want to hear your music. Shankar plays, and his fellow musician, Ustad Alla Rakha, plays the tabila, which is a small pair of drums that he plays with his hands, like bongos. Their music starts slow and comforting with its rhythmic beat, but as it builds, it becomes more passionate and intense, as the two musicians seem to battle through the energy of their instruments. It's raining throughout their entire 20 minute set, but we listen until they finish, and we applaud and cheer at the conclusion.

His music did become popular in our country, but Shankar isn't happy with the drug culture of our youth as it's depicted here at this festival, and a year later he distanced himself from the hippie movement. He said we were all stoned, but he did manage to come back two years after that to do "The Concert for Bangladesh" with George Harrison.

Last night at this time, I remember sitting on the grassy plateau. I turn so I can see exactly where I sat with Gail, before all of today's craziness. I know we made a connection, and she was fun to be with, even if it was just for that short time. I can't forget the excitement I got from kissing her and I loved getting to know her, not that I know that much. We were really comfortable with each other. Her presence took my breath away, and she wasn't just pretty, but cool, and fearless, I also remember how she took a good grasp of me this afternoon. I wonder where she is right now. I guess I'm thinking about her because Melanie is due out soon, and she's a big fan.

I look over the field of spectators, but the wonderful colors of the day are now hidden in the misty night, so I might add is Sharon. The darkness is one way to stop me from glancing over in her direction every now and then. The light from the stage only helps cast shades of grays and blacks in the darkness, and I can also make out low, hovering umbrellas over the crowd, while above them I observe the rain coming down. Then I hear,

"Ladies and Gentlemen, Melanie!"

Melanie is pretty much an unknown but has a couple of hits. She never ever played in front of more than 500 people but happens to work in the same building as Woodstock Ventures and asked to be one of the musical performers. She isn't originally scheduled for now, but because of the rain, The Incredible String Band refuses to go on. You can say she's the first solo female artist to play Woodstock, and that's how she got the title, "First Lady of Woodstock." She's doing a half hour set, and all I can think about is Gail, especially during Melanie's song "Beautiful People."

> *"Beautiful people*
> *You live in the same world as I do*
> *But somehow I never noticed*
> *You before today*
> *I'm ashamed to say*
>
> *Beautiful People*
> *We share the same back door*
> *And it isn't right*
> *We never met before*
> *But then*
> *We may never meet again."*

I feel bad for Gail because Melanie doesn't do the song "Brand New Key," and I'm sure she was waiting for that one. The audience lights candles during her performance, and it inspires her to write "Lay Down (Candles in the Rain)." She's described as quirky, bubbly, and upbeat, a free-spirited hippie representing a girl of the '60s. That's how I think of Gail.

At just around midnight, two acts are left, and the next one is Arlo Guthrie, who isn't expecting to be on tonight, so by the time he gets backstage, he's heavily under the influence of drugs. Someone comes up to him and says, "Arlo, you're on." Arlo's answer is "No, see, I'm not here now, man. I'm coming tomorrow."

I don't know this is going on at the time, but what I hear next over the speakers is,

"Welcome, Mr. Arlo Guthrie!"

He has his 12-string guitar and walks out onto the stage. He looks around and knows this is big and goes to the microphone and belts out these now-famous words, "The New York State Thruway is closed, man." Cheers and applause follow. This quote might be even bigger than; "It's a free concert from now on." Arlo's quote echoes in my head, ever since this night, whenever I think of Woodstock.

Arlo's father was folk pioneer Woody Guthrie, and like his father, he can uplift a whole audience, which he does with his opening song "Coming into Los Angeles." He's the singer and songwriter of "Alice's Restaurant," the restaurant where you can get anything you want — except for Alice, but he chooses not to do that song this evening.

Arlo says that someone yells out, "The New York State Thruway is closed, man," at almost every concert he does. Another note, The feature film, *Alice's Restaurant* opens at theaters Tuesday, August 19, four days after his appearance tonight at Woodstock.

It's now 1:00 a.m., and the last performer hits the stage to close out the first day at Woodstock. She's an anti-war protester, as I believe we all are, but she's also a folksinger, which most of us are not. Sometimes she's compared to her fellow folksinger Bob Dylan, only of the female gender. Joan is going on stage tonight, unbeknownst to all of us, that she is 6 months pregnant.

Over the speakers,

"There's nothing you can say, except the fabulous lady, Joan Baez!"

Her first words from the stage are to wish everyone a good morning. Her voice is exceptionally clear and beautiful this night, while her songs are inspiring. She speaks of her husband, David Harris, who is in federal prison for draft evasion. She also told us how he's led a hunger strike behind bars.

She continues down her list of songs, and other than Richie Havens, her time on stage is the longest at just over an hour, ending after an encore of "We Shall Overcome." Earlier in the afternoon, she was told she would be going on last. "That's okay," she said, "maybe by then there won't be such a puny crowd."

It has been raining harder at various times throughout the evening but stays at a constant drizzle as she performs. As she finishes her set, the rainfall increases to a heavier level. We are planning to stay in place, but with the rain coming down harder and a dry tent at our campsite, we decide to head home. People have either left for the night or are bundled up so tightly that it just makes it easier to walk through the audience and up to our campsite. We walk tiresomely to our shelter where we fall asleep in a matter of seconds.

August 16, 1969 (Saturday)

CHAPTER 10: Breakfast with Gail

Our tent is much better keeping out the evening rain than the morning light, and once again, I'm awakened by God's clock. I leave the tent before the others are awake, stretch, and head towards the cornfield for my morning wizz. Just as I get there, Gail is walking out and even though it's early in the morning she still looks good.

"Good morning," I say.

"Good morning," she replies.

"Would you like eggs for breakfast?"

"Sure! But don't forget to wash your hands."

As I head back to the campsite, I past Brian and Sam as they're on their way into the cornfield.

"Good morning," I say.

Sam says, "Morning" and Brian gives a nod.

When I get back to my tent, Gail is sitting in front of her tent watching me. The first thing I do is to pour water over my hands from my canteen and dry them off with a towel. I hold up the towel as I look in her direction, and she gives me two thumbs up, then I start a fire. Brian and Sam return and have cereal. I can see Gail; she's standing with her back to me and with her head poking inside her tent, apparently speaking with the Bearded One. It's a little chilly and I can see why she's wearing jeans. Then, she comes over with some milk in paper cups as I'm scrambling ours eggs.

"Oh! I want fried eggs," she says frowning. "Just kidding."

I then introduce Gail to Brian and Sam.

"I'm impressed that he knows anybody's name out here." Brian says.

Sam adds, "I'm surprised anyone knows his."

Brian and Sam laugh as they leave. The eggs are done and so is the toast, so I put them on plates as she carries the cups of milk to a vacant log, where we plant ourselves.

"You do know my name, right?"

"Glenn?"

"Are you asking me?"

"No! . . . It's Glenn."

"Okay. Did you keep dry last night?" I ask.

"I covered myself up in a plastic sheet that someone gave me."

"We did the same thing, and we stayed until the end, but when it started to rain hard, we came back here. Did you see Melanie?"

"Wait! Wait! Gail says excitedly. I have to tell you what happened I just remembered. I can't believe it. I was walking along the fence by the helicopters, after I saw you at the water, and I ran into Melanie."

"You ran into Melanie?" I repeat. What did you talk about?

"I don't even remember, but she was trying to get in the gate and she didn't have her performer's pass. They didn't want to let her in. They didn't know who she was. One of the guards asked what she sang. I yelled out, she sings, "Beautiful People" and a guard knew the song and asked her to sing it, and she did and he said, "It sure sounds like her, and they let her in.""

"What about you?"

"No, not me, but it was cool."

"Did you see her last night?" I ask.

"Of course I saw her, and she was really good, but I came back to sleep after Arlo's first song."

"Were you bummed that Melanie didn't sing "Brand New Key?"

"I don't know that song," She says.

"How can you not know that song? It's her biggest hit."

"'Beautiful People' is her biggest hit," she corrects me.

I told her I thought about her during that song.

"You did? I might have thought about you too."

She asks how the "Key" song goes, and I try singing it somewhat,

> "I rode my bicycle past your window last night,
> I roller skated to your door at daylight,
> Da da da da da . . . da, da da da da da."

76

She chimes in, "I'm okay alone, but you got something I need."

If I could melt, I would have, and then I stutter, "I, I knew you knew it."

She laughs and says, "Of course I do, You Silly, but please, don't give up your day job."

"Where were you sitting to watch the concert?" I ask.

"No place particular, I moved around."

I drew a circle in the dirt with a branch and told her,

"This is the bowl, here's the stage, and this is where we are now, outside the circle."

I then point inside the circle, "This is where my blanket is when I'm sitting on the field."

She takes the branch and scribbles some Xs on my drawing. "This is the cornfield."

"Yes, that's right," I confirm. "What a messy place that is turning out to be."

Then she moves the branch back and forth over the dirt inside the circle, messing up the drawing.

"That's where I watched from – all over the place."

Then she giggles, hands me her empty plate and cup, and then scampers away. As she does, I turn and watch her go.

The Bearded One emerges from the tent and heads towards the cornfield as Gail enters the tent. I take our paper plates and cups and throw them in the fire. I wash the pan with water from my canteen. Gail pokes her head out of the tent and says, "Thanks, bye. I'll see you later."

She pokes her head back in. I don't think she really means she'll see me later – I think that's just an expression. Anyway, I go fill my canteen once again. As I walk back and pass her tent, I look inside and see her giving a plate of something to the Bearded One.

I walk to Festival Field, which is now covered with moist, colorful blankets and wet plastic sheets. Throughout the whole meadow the people have made their blankets, their homes, and right now many are sleeping because the concert ended so late. There are also a lot of people walking around and eating rolls or having cereal from those little boxes. The sweet smell of bacon and eggs is in the air coming from the campsite areas where you are allowed to have a gas stove. That's where the real campers set up. The smell of marijuana also fills the early morning air.

The ground is still damp from last night's rain and has mixed with the morning dew, but the sun is shining, and the warmth starts to cover all of us. I see a girl and two guys standing around their sleeping bags.

"How are ya, eh? One guy asks me.

"Doing' good," I answer.

"It's so worth coming here, eh? We drove down from Canada, straight away, got here at night."

"More like morning?" the second guy says.

"You're right," eh? "We decided to come here after suppa and got here aboot 2:00 a.m., that was Friday, eh?"

"Didn't hit any traffic," the girl says, "until we passed the town and then, we hit some. "We followed a Volkswagen mini van, with flowers and peace signs on it, so we knew we were going in the right direction."

"Where in Canada are you guys from?" I ask. "I met some Canadians from Calgary on Thursday."

"From Cowtown, eh? We aren't from that far away. We drove down from Montreal, its almost directly north, eh!"

"Isn't that where John Lennon had the bed-in earlier this year?" I ask.

The girl agrees, and says she tried to see him. She's obviously a big fan of John's.

"John actually wanted to have the bed-in in New York," I say.

"It's funny," the second guy says. Here we are smoking marijuana, and John has a conviction for possession and can't even enter your country."

"Funny . . . or ridiculous?" the girl asks and then answers. "I think it's ridiculous but that's why he's not here, because he can't enter the country."

"I heard The Beatles got an invitation to come, eh? But they declined. Didn't have time to get together, eh?"

"I'm pretty sure," I say, "that if he were in this country, he would be here. He might not have come with the Beatles, but he would have come with Yoko. I'm going with her theory that he's having trouble getting into the country."

That, sort of finishes the conversation.

Jim Morrison was another artist who didn't show, as he thinks someone might take a shot at him and that's why he doesn't play at any outdoor arenas, although John Densmore from Jim's group The Doors is here. Tommy James and the Shondells got this message; "There's a pig farmer in upstate New York who wants you to play in his field." They pass, but James later said, "We could have kicked ourselves." Frank Zappa declined after hearing the weather report, he didn't wish to be in such a muddy place, and Ian Anderson of Jethro Tull declined because of his concerns of inappropriate nudity. Led Zeppelin's manager thinks they would just seem like another band in the mix and thought they're bigger than that.

I'm walking around aimlessly when I come across another group passing a joint around, and the one holding it makes eye contact with me. She gestures for me to take the joint from her hand. We talk about the New York State Thruway being closed, but she says she was already off the highway and parked somewhere on the smaller road in between here and Bethel.

It's always nice just stopping in a crowd and making acquaintances. An offer of a joint is always a sign of welcome, but sometime, so is a simple "Good morning," or "Hell-o," especially if the person has an accent, like those Canadians I had just met earlier.

As I continue walking through the audience, I can see movement on the stage. The microphone gives screeching feedback before a voice speaks,

> "The Daily News is still eight cents. Saturday, August 16, 1969. In large headline, TRAFFIC UPTIGHT AT HIPPIEFEST. There is a picture of the highway with the usual three lanes, but with cars and trucks on both sides of the shoulders, and the traffic is at a standstill five lanes across. The bottom has a sub headline, 'Go-Go is a No-No,' and the article speaks of traffic blues being for

squares, and how traffic is also a jam session that we here are not worried about."

That sure is true for me. I'm not a square, and I'm not worried. Here comes the voice we recognize, Chip,

> "Dr. Jack Somebody. Please come with full surgical equipment. Your presence is required. You got a baby to delivery."

Just for the record, no babies have ever been given credibility for having been born here at Woodstock, regardless of this announcement. All I heard is that someone had a baby at a local hospital, but not here on the farm. I further learned it's just a ploy to have something exciting like a birth at Woodstock to furthering the whole idea that we are a city and that anything can happen, even a newborn.

The helicopters make it harder to hear on stage than out here in the field, but now more copters are present. The aircraft from the previous day are delivering the musical artists for the concert, but here's Chip, over the speakers, to explain the others,

> "Some of you may have noticed our familiar colored helicopter over there. The United States Army has lent us some medical teams. They're with us, man, they're not against us. They are with us and deserve a hand. There are 45 doctors or more, I know at least 45, volunteering their time at the hospital tent, that are here without pay because they dig what this is all about, so if people need help, get to the tent. It's on the far right side of the stage. If you're looking at me, it's on the left.

Those other crafts are from the military and are dropping supplies, such as food, clothing, and toiletries. Governor Rockefeller declared this place a disaster area, allowing the government to step in and help. One helicopter drops flowers, lots and lots of flowers.

Chip continues,

> "Natalie, your mother, Sunshine, is at the food tent. Please head that way Natalie. If you can't find it, ask around for a member of the Hog Farm, they'll guide you there."

Let me just add that the Governor threatens to send in National Guard troops to break up the festival when he sees all the hippies that are here, but John Roberts assures the Governor that everything is going fine and under control. John fears if troops come, there would be a very different atmosphere to the festival, especially if the troops are sent to end it. The Governor tells John the responsibility is now his and refrains from sending any troops, but we do thank him for all the supplies. He's also the one with the credit for closing the highway that Arlo Guthrie mentioned, but I really think it closed itself once cars, buses, and trucks couldn't move anymore.

CHAPTER 11: Dumb Girls

I continue stepping through the crowd and decide to head back to my turf to see Brian and Sam. I trade "Good mornings" with the other Woodstock veterans that made it through the rainy night. I see Sharon talking with Ken. She waves to me and Ken turns around to see who she is waving at. Once he sees me I decide to wave back, but I'm not really smiling. I think she's just teasing me, but why? She starts to get up but Ken tugs her hand to sit back down and she does. I wonder what she would have said? When I get to the blankets, I see Brian and Sam and acknowledge them, they return the greeting with a nod.

Denise is there with her two friends whom I don't know, and who I forgot were gonna be here. Denise is trying to sit down without wrinkling her pants, while the other two girls are sitting with their legs stretched out in front of them. "Good morning," I say. I hear three "Good mornings" back. Denise introduces me to her friends, Mary Ann and Ruthie.

Denise is wearing a new pair of blue paisley bellbottoms with a patchwork leather jacket and large circle-rimmed sunglasses. She has on blue boots to match her pants.

Mary Ann is in calf-high white boots with a bright, colorful mini-skirt that she keeps pushing down between her legs so no one can look up them and see her panties, which, by the way, are red. She has a metal serpent armband and a colorful headband to match the skirt.

Ruthie has on a long dress that has a wide belt and buckle at the waist, making it look like a two-piece. The large buckle is sporting a peace sign. On top she has on a suede, rawhide-colored, fringe vest and a floppy brown hat. A pair of high boots on her feet and a beaded necklace around her neck.

I told them they look good, but they act like they already know. What I meant to say is that they look clean, too clean to be out here.

So I do ask, "How come you girls look so clean?"

Denise is finally able to sit down.

"Why do you think?" she answers. "We went to our trailer when it started raining yesterday, and we stayed inside the whole time."

"You have a trailer?" I ask, not being terribly surprised.

"It's not ours, it's a friend's that we came with."

"Where is he now?" I ask.

"Oh, I don't know. "Denise says. "We don't hang out with him."

"Why don't the groups start playing?" Ruthie asks.

"I think they start at noon today," Brian replies.

"I'm just asking why not now?"

"I'm sure there's a schedule," Brian continues, "and they're probably just waking up, or eating, or maybe still sleeping."

Ruthie isn't even listening to his assumption, and I wonder what they're even doing here. They're dressed like they're going to a nightclub down in Manhattan.

"I don't even see any good-looking guys," Mary Ann says.

"Well," Ruthie continues, "it just seems to me that someone

can be up there playing. We're just sitting around."

"I saw some shirtless guy who looked fine, but his hair was all straggly," Denise says, responding to Mary Ann.

I think to myself, he was probably in the rain all night, not like you prima donnas. I sit down on the other side of Brian and Sam and ask Brian to light up. He whispers, "Not now." A strange answer to my request, but I had a few hits on the way here, so it's fine.

The sun is already warming us up. It's drying our clothes and blankets as well. I think to myself, I should sunbathe nude and get some color.

"Hey, Girls, would you mind if I sunbathe in the nude?" I ask, just trying to be considerate. There's no reply, so I repeat the request louder, "Would anybody mind if I took off my clothes and get some sun?"

"Go ahead," I hear a girls voice answer. Not another sound from the other two girls, so I proceed to take off my clothes, which doesn't consist of much.

Another announcement inquiring about people,

"Mark Abramson, Mark Abramson! Davy needs the car keys desperately. Meet him at the right side of the stage, right side of the stage over there. Steve Berger, Steve Berger! Meet Bill at the information booth, now!"

As I lay on my blanket, my body is completely giving in to the warmth of the sun. My mind relaxes as I find myself thinking about Gail and the first night by the fire and under the stalks of corn. I can see her face with her smile and those glossy eyes. The heat continues to warm my face, and I can feel myself smiling as I think of her down by the pond, taking me by surprise. Boy, was

I startled. She's got nerve, that one. Breakfast with her this morning was nice and very unexpected. She's really sweet. Maybe I'll see her again tomorrow morning, I hope. I start humming, "Beautiful People."

"Glenn!" I hear my name called. Is that Gail? "Glenn!" the voice says again. I sit up, opening my eyes.

"What?" I answer seeing it's not Gail at all.

It's Brian, facing me as I come to realize my surroundings.

"The girls," Brian conveys to me, "would like it if you put your clothes back on."

"What?"

"They feel uncomfortable," he adds.

"Well, I asked them," I say a little agitated.

"I know, I know," he says," but they asked me to talk to you."

"Fine! I don't know why I even bothered to ask," I say frustrated.

Actually, I'm more upset that he disturbed my pleasant dreaming than having to get dressed. So I just put my pants back on and lie back down as another announcement comes over the speakers,

"Insulin and all the other drugs are available in the medical center. If you need something, for God's sake, don't just sit there. You can always come back. We're gonna be here."

CHAPTER 12: Max Yasgur

It's almost 10:00 a. m. I can't light up, and I can't sunbathe, and I don't want to be around these dumb girls. They're not even dressed to be out here, they're dressed to go to some pretentious hippie party where they will frown on hippies getting high. So I get up to see where I might go to get away for a while. It takes me all of one minute when I see a couple of guys a few blankets away, smoking and listening to their radio. So I walk over and ask if I could join them and I learn their names are Billy and Jimmy.

"Are you guys doing alright?" I ask.

"Yeah, man!" Billy says.

"We got here early," Jimmy says, "like 2:00 a.m. and walked from really far to get here, man. Not sure where we parked, but it's 38 signs back. I counted the signs as we passed them, so we'll be able to find our truck when we leave."

"Hey!" Billy says. "We didn't come here in a truck."

"No? Are you sure?"

"Yeah, I'm sure. We came in my dad's car, man. We parked behind a truck. Don't you remember, man?"

"Oh yeah." Jimmy recalls. "The truck was in front of us and had the license plate XE – something 38. We both parked and walked together. They were from Colorado. I thought I was counting signs."

"That's because they had some dynamite weed. They turned

us on as we walked together. You weren't counting any signs. You were counting cars, steps people, anything, you just wanted to count."

"I like to count, it makes the walk go quick; but I didn't count signs?"

"No Jimmy, there weren't enough signs to count. Then we watched the sunrise."

"Oh, yeah! It took 125 seconds till it got in full view."

"You guys must be tired," I interrupt.

"Yeah," Jimmy says, "we must be . . . are we Billy?"

Before Billy can answer he turns the volume on the radio up and we hear the morning news.

> "The place in up-state New York where they are holding that rock festival is becoming an instant big city. It has no conveniences, few police, but no evidence of any violence, not one argument even though there was a twelve-hour traffic jam. I can't even speculate on what it would be like if 450,000 well-dressed businessmen were thrown together in a similar situation. There is marijuana and music at the site, but let it be noted there is no rioting. The young hippies are so packed and jammed in, they can't get proper food or water or adequate medical help. The good humor of the kids is getting them through, but it's a strange way of seeking enjoyment. What's not happening at Yasgur's Farm may be more significant than what is. Let's see how this all plays out and what they say at the end."

Then came the next news story,

"Hurricane Camille and its winds are estimated to have reached 190 miles per hour. The hurricane flattened nearly everything along the coast of the state of Mississippi. People are without—"

Billy changes the radio knob to another station, one with music.

"I think I'll be on my way, I tell them. "Thanks for the news."

Billy says, "Goodbye," but Jimmy is sleeping.

So I say to Billy, "He must be counting sheep now."

As I walk away, Chip makes another announcement,

"I want to get to a warning that I've received. You may take it with as many grains of salt you wish. It's that the brown acid that is circulating around us is not specifically good. It's suggested that you do stay away from that, but it's your trip so be my guest, but please be advised that there is a warning on that acid. If you must try it, consider only half."

After that he did some personal ads,

"Cha Cha from Minnesota, please meet Lisa at the information booth, now. Whoever knows Wheat Germ Holly, she has your bag with your medicine, so please meet at the information booth as soon as you can."

And lastly, for the time being some general information,

"The situation at the top of the hill is that food is being sold at cost. There's also food being served for free on the other side of the wooded area at the Hog Farm. Buses to the Monticello area are also leaving hourly."

I'm not interested in any buses, but the Hog Farm caught my attention. I have an idea and head back to my blanket.

"Brian!"

"What!"

"Do you think we will need that can of beans I brought?"

"Are you kidding?" he answers sarcastically. "If Sam eats them, we'll never be able to sleep in our tent. Why do you wanna know?"

"I'm thinking of taking it to the Hog Farm."

"Sure. It's yours anyway."

"That's not true, it's ours," I remind him.

"Is everything ours?" he asks.

"Yes, Brian, everything is ours."

"Then can I have breakfast with Gail tomorrow?"

"Why don't you invite Denise, although you will probably have to go to her trailer and serve her breakfast in bed."

Denise speaks up, "Did someone say breakfast in bed?"

"No, Denise," We both answer in unison.

I maneuver my way amidst the crowd till I get back to the campsite. I'm hoping that maybe Gail will be there, but I look around, but the flap to her tent is closed, so no luck. I go into my tent and pick up the can of beans that now reminds me of Sharon. She probably wants to be friends now; just friends, so I'll be glad to get rid of this can, and hopefully not see Sharon any more.

I'm heading pass the area of the woods that Brian, Sam, and I had walked into and out of yesterday, much further down in this direction is the road that brought us here. As I venture on Yasgur's property, I see an Arts and Crafts Fair, but I don't stop. I see a long line at the phone booths and even longer lines at the toilets. Then, I see the information booth, and not far from that is an abandoned ticket booth, which sits in front of an entrance, at least it appears that it would have been an entrance, if they had finished constructing the fences.

I think this could have actually been the main entrance because this is the main paved road off Highway 90. We took it, but turned on another paved road that led us to the cornfield parking lot. Some parking lots are up this road before you get to this point, so travelers would park there and head right to this entrance, but with no fences they're just entering everywhere. This road actually passes me and leads behind me down to the Pavilion where I met Jerry Garcia.

The information booth is open, so I ask where the Hog Farm is, not just to see what is going on there, but I also have a delivery to make. I'm directed to follow a white fence. I start on my way and then all of a sudden,

"Hi Glenn."

I turn around, "Hi Sharon." What are you doing here at this childish festival?" I say sarcastically.

She moves forward to kiss me, but I turn so all she kisses is my cheek.

"Ken wanted to come and I did have my ticket, but really after you left I missed you. I wanted to find you. I can't believe all the people, but we made it and I was so excited when I saw you. I never thought I would once I saw this crowd".

"What about your new boyfriend Ken?" I ask. "I thought you like him now."

"Oh! It took me just a day to realize I like you much more and I'm sorry. I made a mistake."

"So what do you expect me to do now?"

"I want you to come back to camp after this," she says. "I want you back. I don't like seeing you sitting with those girls. I'm a little jealous."

"What are you going to do with me," I ask, "hide me in your bunk?"

"No! I over heard the management talking, they were mad at the kitchen boss for firing you."

"No! I quit," I say a little angrily.

"Well, she continues, "I know they will take you back and so will I."

Then she moves forward to kiss me again, and I don't turn away this time.

"Glenn, come back, please," she says in a cutesy kind of way. Then adds, "What are you doing with that can of beans?

"It's a long story."

"Well, I'm going back to sit with Ken, we have to get back to camp tonight, but I'll be waiting for you there." She kisses my on the lips again and I kiss back.

"Bye!"

"Bye!" I say back.

Wow! I can get back my job and my girl, and I'm here enjoying the concert. Right on!

As I continue en route to the Hog Farm I find the fence and it surrounds what looks like, even to a city boy like myself, a cow pasture with a huge red barn. Alongside the barn is a silo that stands almost twice as high as the barn itself.

As I walk along the white fence, I see a small number of hippies gathering. The man in charge looks about 50-years-old and appears to be out of place because most hippies are young, wearing t-shirts, or old with long hair and long beards. He's wearing black slacks and a white button-down short-sleeve shirt. His hair is short, and he's clean-shaven. He has on a pair of dark rimmed glasses and is puffing on a pipe. He surely isn't a hippie, but he has my attention because he is directing other people to hand out water to the small circle of thirsty hippies. Something else catches my eye. The water is in milk bottles strangely enough, and then, I remember we are on a dairy farm. Can that possibly be Max Yasgur?

I decide to shout out,

"MAX!"

He turns and looks at me as I walk over to him.

"Yes, son, you need some water?" he asks.

"No sir, . . . thank you though. I have a canteen right here."

I don't know where the "sir" came from, but it seems appropriate. I continue, "Are you Mr. Max Yasgur?"

"Yes, but I thought you knew that when you called out my name."

"I saw the milk bottles and took a guess. I couldn't imagine it would really be you."

He took in some smoke from his pipe and then blew it out.

"I heard," he says, "that some of the local residents are selling water. Dammit! How can anyone ask money for water?"

"I heard that, too."

"Those town people don't like this whole thing. After I leased my land to that Michael Lang fella, a sign was posted, 'Stop Max's Hippie Music Festival. No 150,000 hippies here.'"

"That sucks."

"I don't particularly like your lifestyle with the drugs and free love, but Americans in uniforms give their lives in war time so you kids can do exactly what you want. I don't agree with those town people. They never wanted you kids here, but this is America, and I wasn't going to give in to them."

"Mr. Yasgur, sir, I really appreciate it and so do a lot of other hippies here today. We can't thank you enough. May I shake your hand, sir?"

I shift the can of beans to my left hand. Max put the pipe up to his mouth, and his right hand took hold of my right hand with a firm grip and gives it a good shakin'. When he finishes, he removes the pipe from his mouth.

"Well then . . . What's your name, young fella?"

"Glenn . . . Glenn Eldridge."

"Well, Glenn," he says, "I made a deal with that Michael fella before the festival, that if anything goes wrong, I'm going to give him a crew cut, and if everything turns out okay, I'm going to let my hair grow long. So you and all your buddies make sure you don't start any trouble."

"But you'll lose the bet."

"Doesn't matter. I'm so bald I'll never be able to grow any hair."

Then he smiles, winks, and puts the pipe back in his mouth as he turns back to the small crowd that had gathered.

"Bye, Max."

He throws his hand up as a farewell gesture, and I'm on my way.

Max sold his farm less than two years later and after another two years he died from a heart attack in 1973 at the age of 53. He was honored with a full-page obituary in Rolling Stone Magazine, which very few non-musicians ever received. Thank you, Max.

CHAPTER 13: The Hog Farm

I came upon the area where the Hog Farm is set up, and that's also where the "free stage" has been erected. The free stage doesn't have any of the big names, but has local bands, mimes, jugglers, poets, and speakers throughout the weekend in the hopes of entertaining some of the crowd.

I cross the small grassy area and sit down in the audience, and I can see the stage is full of cymbals. On the right side of the stage are just cymbals on stands like the ones drummers use, but no drums. There are about 10 of them, and the rest of the stage has 5 different size gongs like the ones they hit with mallets in China. Amazingly, there is only one person playing them all. Behind the stage, I see two psychedelic colored buses acting as the backdrop. The guy next to me is smoking a joint, and hands it to me. When the song is over, he starts telling me that The Merry Pranksters built this stage, and they came in those buses. He tells me Joan Baez had played here yesterday afternoon, way before her performance on the main stage. A second song is being played on the cymbals, but sounds very much like the first one. So I thank him, get up with my can of beans, and proceed to head towards the feeding tents.

It's easy to tell this is the food distribution center because I can smell the food. I also know because the information booth gave me exact directions. It's really great that this is here because no one realized a half million people were gonna show up just to hear some folk and rock music. Everyone here probably thought there would be concession stands available, but even if there were, I suspect they would have run out of food by Friday evening just like the few that are here. Many of the visitors that have come are eating thanks to this food center, but there are many other people sharing their own food.

The food being served isn't really under a tent, but a canvas that hangs horizontally over the long tables that are set up with paper plates, cups, and plastic utensils. It protects the food from the rain and makes a great landmark, letting the hungry people know where they can get food.

I'm not even that close when I found myself at the end of the food line, and before I can step away, hungry hippies are lining up behind me. I'm not here to take food, I'm here to drop off food, but as I'm about to step out of line I hear,

"Hey! Would you like me to hold your place in line? I'm Willow."

"Hi, I'm Glenn. Thanks, but I shouldn't even be in this line. I'm just here to see what's going on and donate this can of beans. Did you come here with any food?"

"We were gonna buy food in Bethel, but we had to park our car on the side road just before we entered the city. Everyone was walking, so we took what we could and walked through the town. We got into the center of town about midnight, and there were people sleeping in front of the stores, so we continued to come straight here."

"From what I heard, the stores in town emptied pretty quickly," I say.

"When we got here," Willow says, "we immediately asked about food and were told about the food tents on the hill. So we went there first, and the lines weren't too long because the sun was just rising, but we still waited for about a half hour once they opened. That was Friday, and now the place has no food."

"So you heard about the Hog Farm?"

"No, not yet," she says. "On the other side of those food tents, was a carnival, and there were a lot of families with their kids."

"I was very surprised there were kids here at all," I say.

"Well, there are a lots of them at the carnival, but we decided to take a ride on the Ferris wheel anyway before we left that area."

"Ferris wheel?" I ask surprised. "Are you kidding?"

"No, but anyway we were on line at the Ferris wheel when we heard about the Hog Farm, and I'm glad because we didn't know where we were gonna get our next meal. The ride was fun, and from the top, we could see the Hog Farm food tents we were told about.

"Did you find the water lines?" I ask. "If not, you can get some water down there by the red barn."

"Yes! That's where I got some water, but now I'm hungry."

By now, the line had move substantially closer to the food, and we continue talking.

"There are a lot of people here," I say, "so there's gonna be long lines all weekend. I've been here since Thursday and I think at this point no newcomers are gonna be close enough to walk here anymore."

"I heard this place is considered a disaster area," Willow says, "because of some governor."

"Yeah! Governor Rockefeller."

Willow continues, "Yes, that's him, he said it's because

there's little food, lack of medical help, and not enough bathrooms, but I don't know exactly what that means."

"Well, it's a good thing, Willow. It means the U.S. government can intervene and bring in supplies, food, and medical personal, which they have already started to do."

"That's great."

We're getting closer to the food table, and the line is full of very hungry people. The line behind us is even longer than when I first got here. We can see the hippies, who just got their food, and no one is complaining about the portions, and everyone seems happy. I'm still talking to Willow when her friend pops in line behind us.

"Hey, Willow!"

"Hi," she answers.

"Who's your friend?" he asks.

"Oh! This is Glenn, and this is who I came with, Wolf.

"Hi, how you doing, Glenn?" he asks suspiciously.

He sounds a little protective of Willow, but I'm not completely sure. He has ears that come to a point on top, not rounded like ears usually are. His sideburns also come to a point, facing downward. If you think I'm gonna ask him why he's called Wolf, you are sadly mistaken.

"Fine, what's up with you?" I reply.

"I was at the concert. Some group came on called Quill. I'd never heard of them and didn't like the music once they started playing, so I thought I'd leave and find my girl, Willow."

"I guess it's after noon," I say. "At least the concert started on time today."

We could hear Quill faintly in the background, now that the performers on the free stage are between acts. We are close to the front of the line where the table is.

"What are you doing with those beans?" Wolf asks.

"I'm actually donating them to the Hog Farm."

A girl standing by the line hands me a joint, and I take one or two hits and hand it to Wolf, who quickly takes it and says, "Thanks, man," in a less mistrusting voice than he had just a moment ago. He hands the joint to Willow, who passes it back to me without taking a hit. I hand it back to the girl who was kind enough to share and then step out of line. I was only here to talk to Willow while we got closer to the food tables and we were almost upon them.

I can see a person chopping up vegetables and another stirring up soup. Then, I see the same guy, who I had seen twice yesterday— once walking around the grounds with his kazoo, and once at the medical tent helping Bob, who was on that bad acid trip. Now he's at the food center. Who is this guy?

He's coming out from behind the table, but looks like he may be in charge. He's giving instructions to one of the others servers before he slips out right next to me. I say, "Hi," and he turns to me.

"I have this can of beans I'd like to donate if it's alright."

"Of course it's alright," he says.

I hand it to him, and he goes to the table and puts it down. He calls out to Lisa that some food has been donated, and a girl comes and takes the can off the table and back with her. Meanwhile, Willow and Wolf are at the table getting their plates.

"Willow! Wolf! Nice meeting you guys."

They both hold up peace signs.

The man once again walks by me and thanks me again for my donation.

"Hi, I'm Glenn," introducing myself. "I think what you're doing is great."

He looks at me with his almost toothless smile.

"Hi, I'm Hugh, how do you do?"

"I saw you at the medical tent yesterday, helping someone who was tripping."

"Oh yeah!" he says. "That was Bob. He was on that brown acid. Once he knew his own name, it helped me get a little control over his situation. You just got to let him know you understand and that he's just to high, but that he's safe until he comes down. Once he was down, we waited about an hour before turning him into a doctor, or at least someone who can help others experiencing the same thing."

"It's a great system," I say.

"It's been working well."

"Are you part of the Hog Farm?"

"Yes, you can say that."

"How did they get that name, Hog Farm?

"That's an interesting story. There were about 40 of us, and we had just lost our place in California. A neighbor came by and told us that some guy in the mountains had a stroke, and he needed someone to feed, wash, and take care of his hogs. It was a rent-free place on a mountain, and all we had to do was take care of 45 hogs. That's how the Hog Farm got started. That was about four years ago. So you could say I've been part of the Hog Farm since day one."

"How'd you wind up here?"

"We were in New York," he says, "and had just rented land in New Mexico when we were approached by Woodstock Ventures and asked if we would help at this festival. I told them we were going to New Mexico, but they offered to jet us back here for this festival. So this past week, we were loaded onto a jet and flown here. There are about a hundred of us and when we arrived, the press addressed us as the security. That was funny, so we called ourselves the 'Please Force.' We control situations by saying, 'Please do this and please don't do that.' We made walking trails and built fire pits, but we also convinced the promoters to let us set up this free kitchen."

"That was a good idea." I confirm. "I don't know what would happen if hungry people had no place to get food. This line has only gotten longer since I've been here.

"Exactly. By the way, can you help out for a short time? I'm needed at the trip tent, I mean the medical tent and just need someone to help dish out food while I'm gone. I'll get back as soon as I can."

"Sure! I'd like to lend a helping hand, and I appreciate you talking with me."

"We appreciate the beans."

He takes me to the front of the line, helps me slip behind the table and tells the others it's okay. He tells me again that his name is Hugh, he'll be back in about a half hour, and Lisa is the law. He's really cool to spend that time with me when he has so much to do. Now, I can help out in some little way, so I pick up the spoon to start serving, and then I can't believe my eyes.

By the way, he was trying to be funny when he said, "Lisa is the law." That is her name, Lisa Law and she's a photographer, but is helping feed people here at Woodstock.

CHAPTER 14: We Meet Again

The folksinger who's now on the free stage sounds really good, and the sun is shining, but not in my eyes since I'm under the canvas ready to dish out food. Hugh was more than generous with his time, and now, I'm about to help serve food to my fellow hippies when I notice the girl besides me serving the chow isn't the same girl who was serving it before. She's swaying her hips and humming, and I know her, "Hi." She turns towards me – it's Gail, and she looks right in my eyes with her own glossy ones, and says, "Yeah, I guess I am." I laugh, but soon learn she's not kidding as she hands me a joint that's in her other hand. She is pretty stoned also, which is a give away by her slow speech.

"How did you find me?" she asks.

"If you mean this morning, I found you quite entertaining."

"No, You Silly, how did you find me here?"

"I asked some hippies if they've seen a pretty girl in jeans."

"You did not," she says. "Did you, really?"

"I did, and they asked me if I was blind."

She looks up with glazed eyes and a faraway stoned smile and says, "You're funny."

"Actually, I wasn't looking for you. I just wanted to get away from three horrid girls at my blanket."

"You were with three girls, huh? And you had to come find

me? Are you saying it takes three girls to equal me? I like that."

In my head I'm thinking, "There are no girls that can equal you, and it's pure luck I found you at all, and I'm so glad I did." But the only words that come out of my mouth were . . .

"I had this 5lb. can of beans I wanted to get rid of."

Oh, that had to be the stupidest thing I've ever said, and I quickly changed the subject. "How did you get to be a server?"

"I heard about the Hog Farm yesterday and helped them before the concert started. Today, I thought I would help again, so I came down here after giving breakfast to my cousin."

Suddenly a good warm feeling rushed through my body, and it's not from the pot. I'm not sure what I heard would change anything, but I want to make sure I heard her correctly, before I assume anything.

"Oh! You came with your cousin?"

"Yes, we came here together after he picked me up at the airport."

"I mean . . . are you two more . . . more together?"

"What do you mean, more together?" she asks.

Then she looks at me oddly and gasps, "Owww! No, not like that. What gave you that crazy idea?"

"I thought maybe because you were down at the lake skinny-dipping with him."

"First of all, he's seen me naked before, and secondly, if I remember, even though you pretended not to look, you saw me naked too. Third, I wasn't naked. I had on panties."

"Pink! I mean . . . I really didn't notice."

"Lastly," she says, "if you remember, there was a part of me that was interested in a part of you."

"Oh!" I say. "That was on purpose?"

I only asked that way so I wouldn't seem as stupid as I'm now appearing to be.

She moves in close and kisses me on my lips, and her tongue starts sneaking into my mouth. I'm thinking we have people to feed, but it feels nice and I don't really want to stop, I'm figuring it won't take long, but—.

"Hey, guys!" Hugh interrupts. "I know kissing builds up your mouth, but you're supposed to be feeding these people."

Our lips part, and I'm staggering a little from the kiss.

"That was fast," I say.

"They didn't need me after all, but I'm glad I came back. These people are starving, and you're playing around. Why don't you guys take a break?"

As we come around the table, I can see him smiling, he's missing his front teeth, almost all of them, I hadn't noticed that before, and then he gives Gail a wink. His reaction to her makes me feel like the whole thing was a set-up, but I'm probably wrong. Well, anyway it was great news about the Bearded One being her cousin. When we get away from the food tent and the crowd around it, I turn to her, hold both her arms down at her sides and give her a quick kiss on the lips and say, "I just didn't like the way that other kiss ended," and her stoned face now breaks into an even bigger smile.

We start walking away from this area and we find ourselves on the back end of the wooded area. I tell her about the bridge in the woods, which we had taken and how we were so stoned we didn't realize we were going in a circle till we got off. I tell her about the three girls back at my blanket and how they didn't like the way I was sunbathing. She tells me it wouldn't have bothered her, but I already guessed that. She tells me she saw Joan Baez sing on the Free Stage yesterday while she was dishing out food. She said that was after she saw Melanie.

"Looks like there's a tent on this side of the woods," I say.

"Let's check it out."

This area is designated as "Movement City." We go inside and the people are handing out pamphlets and want to discuss politics. They want to talk about how bad our government is and what we should do to change it. There are a few different radical groups here, and it's very pleasing to me that Gail is as uninterested in these people as I am. As we are leaving a guy follows us out of the tent and approaches us to try and sell us drugs. Not just marijuana, but hashish, LSD, and mescaline. Again, I'm happy to see she's not interested in any of that either. We learn later that this is definitely an unofficial and unlawful use of the grounds.

We continue our walk, and this path leads us past an area where a bunch of tents have been set up. A community group has traveled here with maybe 50 people, and they're residing in this area. As we walk through, it's like "Hippie Haven" with all the hippies here in colorful garments and they have flowers in the hair while the young ones run around half naked. We stop and talk to a woman named Crystal holding a baby. She tells us that they consider themselves one big family. They work together, share money, and have this unconventional lifestyle outside of Woodstock. They do theater acting or musical interludes as a way of raising money. She tells us some of their followers are performing in the direction we are heading.

We pass some self-proclaimed musicians; a couple – one is playing the flute while the other one is banging on a drum. They might have been the ones at the bonfire our first night here, who knows. Gail and I are walking close to one another, and occasionally our hands bump. I'm aware of each touch, but haven't gotten the nerve to grab her hand yet. I was hoping she would just grab mine, but I gave up that thought once I remember that she isn't as shy as I am—after all she grabbed what she wanted yesterday, so I assume if she wants to grab my hand, she will.

Once we pass the music, we eye the theatrical group that Crystal mentioned and walk over to watch. These are the same girls I saw yesterday, dressed like Indian squaws with their patches of cloth. One stands alone right now pretending to pick petals off a daisy, repeating, "He loves me . . . he loves me not . . . he loves me . . . he loves me not," as the expressions on her face alternates with the feeling she gets from each pull of a petal. Then, another Indian squaw gets into the performance area, doing the same thing and then another. As I tell Gail I saw them yesterday, she jumps in on the act. She has a very big smile as she picks off one make-believe petal and cries, "he loves me." Then, like a sad faced clown, she whimpers, "he loves me not," she continues with "he loves me," excitedly.

"Stop right there," I yell.

"But, I have three petals left."

"Well, you can do two more, but that's it."

She makes believe she's throwing the flower away and rushes to me and gives me a big hug. We continue our walking and we hear a loud roar from the crowd at The Bowl, and she says, "Let's go see who's playing now."

When we get there, we look out over the wonderful field of people, and there is one person standing in the middle of the stage. I'm not sure who it is at first, not until I recognize the song.

"I think that's Country Joe." I say.

"And the Fish?" she asks.

"No! It looks like he's playing solo, and I know that song. It's called "Janis," and he wrote it about Janis Joplin. You know he actually dated her for a while."

"I didn't know that," she says, "but I really like her music."

We continue walking.

"I really do love Janis; she's my favorite singer."

"I thought Melanie was your favorite singer."

"She was . . . yesterday, but I saw her, and now I want to see Janis. I can like many people, you know, I like you."

"But I don't sing," I say jokingly.

"True, but I like the way you hold me sometimes."

"Not all the times?"

"No, just some times."

Then she gives me a quick kiss on the cheek and scampers away as only she can. I chase her a little, then, we start walking together again. It's little after 1:00 p.m., when we arrive back at the campsite.

I ask her if she wants a PB&J sandwich, and she nods her head yes, before heading back into her tent and says she'll just be a minute.

I go into my tent to get the bread and the two other ingredients to make the sandwiches. When I finish making them, I wait in front of my tent for her to show because I don't want to be rude and start eating without her. She comes out of the tent having changed out of her long jeans and into a blue simple throw-on dress that hangs loosely past her knees, a thin belt pulling the dress tight at her waist, and a pair of light brown moccasins with those little beads around them. A plain light blue headband makes her hair bunch up on top but it sprouts straight out from underneath. Her face has a smile on it, not showing her teeth and I can't help but tell her,

"You look beautiful."

"Some of those hippies you talked to were right," she says.

"Which ones?"

"The ones who said you were blind."

"Don't you know how to take a compliment?" I ask.

"Not really, but I'll try, say it again."

"Don't you know how to take a—"

"No! Not that, You Silly."

"I know, I know," I said smiling. "You look beautiful."

"Thank you," she responds.

"I hope you like the sandwich I made for you."

I hand her the plate with the sandwiches.

"What would you like to wash it down with?" I ask.

"What do we have?"

I love the "we" part. "Water, milk, or wine?"

"How about wine?"

"I'll get a bottle and two cups."

"We don't need no stinking cups."

She goes and sits on the same log that we sat on for breakfast, and I come back with the wine.

"Good sandwich," she says.

She proceeds to wash it down with a large mouthful of wine.

"It's not a contest," I say.

"It's hard to swallow peanut butter without a drink."

"I just want you to save some for me."

We head to the concert and, in a way, I want to show her off to those three dumb girls, but in another way, it just doesn't matter.

Instead of telling you about other groups that didn't want to come let me introduce to you three groups that were scheduled to perform and didn't show up. I know this because their names are on the purple Wallkill poster. The Jeff Beck Group (Featuring Rod Stewart) had broken up a week before the festival. Beck later said he regretted it. The Moody Blues backed out after booking the same weekend in Paris. Iron Butterfly were left at the airport because the crowd was doing so well, there was fear that bringing in a heavy metal band might trigger some violence or incite a riot.

CHAPTER 15: Santana

We maneuver our way through the crowd. Country Joe is still on stage and starts his "Fish" cheer, but he doesn't spell fish.

"Give me an F," he demands.

The crowd responds with the appropriate letter.

"Give me a U," he says next.

The crowd continues to call out,

"Give me a C."

And then, to round out the word, he asks for a 'K.'"

"What's that spell?" he asks.

The crowd screams, "FUCK."

"What's that spell?"

"FUCK."

"What's that spell?"

"FUCK."

And that continues for three more yells.

Into the song he goes as we get closer to our seats, but before we get there, Country Joe stops singing and starts scolding the audience by saying,

> "Listen, people, I don't know how you expect to ever stop the war if you can't sing any better than that. There are about 300,000 of you fuckers out there. I want you to start singing. Come on."

The crowd claps and cheers, and then he continues,

> *"And it's one, two, three. What are we fighting for?*
> *Don't ask me I don't give a damn, Next stop is Vietnam."*

We reach our seats as Country Joe finishes his Vietnam anti-war song and walks off stage. The roadies come out and start getting the stage ready for the next act. We don't know who will preform next, and we don't care.

Denise and her two friends are gone, and so is most of our bottle of wine. Brian and Sam remember Gail, and Brian tells me that Denise and her friends just left, which would explain him lighting up a joint now. I trade our bottle of wine for a few hits of their joint. Gail and I take a few long hits. We get comfortable on my blanket, and I lean my head on a rolled-up part that acts as my pillow, and she leans her head on my chest. She's on my left side, and I put my left arm around her shoulder.

The announcement simply says,

> "Ladies and Gentlemen, Santana!"

The crowd roars, and I kiss Gail on the top of her head. She turns her head upward to face me with a smile and turns back in place. Santana and his band start playing and bring their sound of mixing Latin music and rock music to Woodstock. He's a San Francisco guitarist, and his debut album has just been released. The strong percussion sound fills the air, and with Santana on the lead guitar, he's taking my thoughts away and replacing them with music.

One story goes that Bill Graham wanted the group he managed, Santana, to perform; Michael Lang wanted It's a Beautiful Day. Bill flipped a coin and Santana won, later it was suspected that Bill had a two-headed coin.

I lie on my back very conscious as my thoughts drifts away to the music. The rhythm is both powerful and soothing, and I would leave my body if I didn't get such pleasure from holding Gail next to me. Feeling her there is very comforting. Her right hand lies quite still, between us, while her left arm rests on my chest. During their set my hand gently rubs her back.

The sun feels warm against my face, and I'm very relaxed. I can feel Gail trying to get the arm in-between us in a more comfortable position. She stops moving, so I guess she found the right spot. The next song takes me away again, but I stay grounded by stroking Gail's hair, and her hand starts rubbing my chest. The movement of our hands on each other is in unison to the sound coming over the speakers, and I feel we are enjoying the music almost as one. The bongos help the flow of the song, and being stoned doesn't hurt either. At the end of the song, the audience cheers and applauds. Michael Shrieve is the band's drummer and happens to be the youngest musician to play at Woodstock, turning 20 years old just 5 ½ weeks earlier.

Santana speaks,

> "Thank you. Thanks very much. We have one more tune for you. It's called 'Soul Sacrifice.'"

The bongos start once again. I reach out my right hand across my body and lightly brush her cheek, and then my hand falls back to my side. She acknowledges my caress with one of her own. She takes her hand and slides it under my shirt onto my hairless chest.

She moves up along my side until her face is almost next to mine. I can feel her breath on my neck, so I pull her a little closer and turn my head towards her, so we can kiss once again, but the kissing is slow and gentle.

The music surrounds us making the kiss heighten as we communicate through the touching of our lips. My hand is moving up to cup the back of her head as her hand starts moving in a circular motion on my chest and brushes over my nipples. I can feel the throbbing within our bodies, and I pull her headband off letting her hair drape over our faces. I feel at one with her and the music.

Our lips separate, and she edges back down by my side, making it easier for her hand to slide over my stomach. I can feel myself growing firm, pushing against the zipper of my jeans. I can feel myself getting excited as her hand lowers to the top of my jeans, and I flinch and open my eyes as her hand slides down even further, onto my jeans. She turns her head upward to face me with a smile, and her eyes are looking into mine as she whispers, "I know what I'm doing." Her eyes close, and her head turns back down in place as she leans in closer and her hand continues down my jeans. All I can do is close my eyes.

I can feel her hand, her palm applying pressure downward on the bulge inside my pants as it pushes upward trying to break through the fastener. The passion grows with every movement of her hand, and each breath I take, and both are in sync with the incredible sound of Santana's music.

Gail continues to excite me by using her thumb and fingers to wrap around me as best she can through my pants. After throwing my underwear in the garbage yesterday, I went commando today and that only makes the fabric between us one layer less. Her hand holds tightly to the outline of my masculinity as she rubs up and down distinctly to the beat of the music. I'm breathing heavier and turn trying to utter something, but she turns her head upward again and says, "Don't speak, it's okay. I've handled this before."

I can't speak. It feels too good, and it's getting more intense. My fingers are running through her hair, and she's running her hand up and down. I continue to lose myself in the rhythm of the Latin beat and the extreme pleasure she's putting me through. The furthest thing from my mind is that I'm on a blanket surrounded by thousands of people. I'm oblivious to everything around except the sound in my head and the excitement in my pants.

Her hand stops but doesn't loosen its grip, and I know she can feel me throbbing in her hand. She squeezes back, but she must be teasing me. I turn my head towards her as the music is surrounding us, and she looks as if she's in her own little trance. She must know I'm close to exploding because my body is twitching to her every squeeze.

I start stroking her head as her hair falls between my fingers in the hope she'll start rubbing again. She maneuvers her body closer, and her head tilts slightly on my chest to get more comfortable. She starts working the up and down motion once more. Our passion is becoming more intense. Her hand is in control of my excitement and continues applying pressure through my jeans. I start twitching and moaning as she's stroking me through the fabric. I can feel my groin bringing up fluid from deep within as her hand is in total control of the eruption, and the vibrant tempo of "Soul Sacrifice" continues. The music becomes more powerful as her hair flows between my fingers, and her hand is bringing everything to a climax.

Her hair becomes tangled in my clinched fist and my manhood is ready to explode. I hear the familiar song of Santana building to its climax, just as I am. Gail knows it too since her stroking quickens as my body becomes tense. She draws her body tightly into mine and can tell I'm close. I can feel the lava climbing, and I try to hold back, but I can only hold back for seconds. I explode, and my body's quivering and jerking, but Gail holds me tight as if to hang on for the ride. My body is shaking, but she doesn't stop just yet, but chooses to slow the massaging down. She felt the pulsating at its height and is slowly working to bring me back. I can hear the crowd cheering and for a split second, I thought, "They're cheering for me." They're clapping and roaring because the song has ended. I have finished too, but my quivering body needs a little more time to adjust after the intense trip it's been on.

Then I feel raindrops on my face, but I can hardly move. As I try to get up, the rain starts coming down heavier, but Gail pushes me down, grabs a plastic sheet and covers us quickly. She tucks it under me on one side and under herself on the other, and I can hear the patter of the rainfall against the plastic. I don't know what Brian and Sam are doing, but Gail and I are safely covered, keeping dry and falling asleep from pure exhaustion.

Carlos Santana said he had been tripping on mescaline during his performance and he was trying to control his guitar because he was hallucinating that the neck of his guitar was a snake squirming to get free.

CHAPTER 16: John Sebastian

I'm awoken by a voice in the air.

> "There's a cat, and I really don't even know his name, but I remember the Chip said his old lady just had a baby. That kids gonna be far out."

I'm thinking I'm that cat, and what the hell did I do? Based on the last thing I remember before falling asleep I thought somehow I've gone through some time warp and he's talking about me. It has to be the drugs. I come to my senses quickly and open my eyes to find Gail still resting her head on my chest, still asleep and not moving, so I remain still. I know she's knocked out from all the wine, pot, and extracurricular activities. The plastic sheet is bundled up at our side.

The voice over the speakers is that of John Sebastian, and he continues to speak,

> "I don't know if you know how amazing you are? Boy! This is really a mind fucker of all times, man. I've never seen anything like this, man. Just love everybody."

Gail gives my hand a squeeze at that moment, so I know she's not asleep.

John continues,

> "And clean up a little garbage on your way out and everything's gonna be alright. My man Chip . . . is doing so well. The press can only say bad things, unless there ain't no fuck-ups, and it's looking like there ain't gonna

be no fuck-up. This is gonna work. Yeah! For you and everybody."

Gail and I sit up, and I can feel the mess in my pants.

"How about we go down to the water?" I ask.

"And miss . . . who's this guy?"

"John Sebastian," I answer. "We'll listen to him as we walk out of here. I'd like to clean myself up."

"Oh yes, you should do that, you never know when it can happen again." She winks at me.

"I don't think it will happen like that again," I say. "The music was so intense."

"Wasn't I intense?" she asks.

"The whole thing was intense," I say. "Didn't you find it intense?"

With a mischievous smile on her face and eyes wide open, she answers, "Yes."

I think to myself, Sharon had done something like that, but nothing close to how good it felt with Gail. I don't care if the whole crowd was watching I just hope Sharon wasn't. I look towards where Sharon is sitting and she's facing the stage, and I continue walking. Gail is a little further in front of me, when I spot Sharon looking my way. She gives me a little wave, a smile and thumbs up. Gail's ahead and doesn't notice my thumbs up back to Sharon. I don't know what to feel, but I can't be rude.

We proceed to get to the pond, and I tell her to sit right on the rocks. She asks what I'm hiding, and I say, "Just sit there!" I go around a tree to get to the water. There are several other hippies in the water, but I'm not interested in looking at anyone else. I put down the canteen and pull my T-shirt over my head, knocking off my bandana again. I pick it up and put it back on . . . again, then lay my shirt across a large boulder because it doesn't need washing and slip off my sneakers. I take off my pants, walk into the water and clean them off. After wringing and smoothing them out I put them on the boulder next to my shirt and canteen. Now I head into deeper water to clean myself.

I'm waist deep and notice Gail's in the water with her back to me, her head looking over her left shoulder as her hair lays straight down her back. I can see her naked bronze tan and the top of her white panties, which are just under the water level.

"I see you're wearing white today," I say.

"I don't have blue ones."

I continue cleaning myself.

She asks, "What are you waiting for?"

Then she plunges under the water and only emerges up to her shoulders, facing me. Her wet brown hair shines, and the reflection of the sun dances off the rippling waves that she has created. I start walking toward her, and she's just waiting for me. She's still only sticking her head out of the water so as not to expose herself further, and I really want to get a better look at her. She has a cute smile, and I'm starting to feel that feeling below the water again, and I'm about three feet away from her.

All of a sudden she jumps up and starts splashing the water at me, and I turn my head to avoid getting splashed in the face. When she stops, I turn to face her and she's gone. She has passed me and is heading towards the shore. As she's walking out of the water I can see her white panties accenting the curves of her behind and then she disappears around the tree, and I slowly walk out of the water and put on my slightly damp jeans. I feel something in the pocket that I forgot I had. I continue putting on the rest of my clothes and adjust my bandana.

I feel clean once more, grab the canteen, and turn the corner around the tree. Gail has her dress back on and is wringing out her panties. She then flaps them in the air getting out the twists and wrinkles and proceeds to slide them on under her dress. She puts on her belt, adjusts her clothes, slides into her moccasins and looks as good as new.

"I have a surprise for you," I say.

"Don't tell me you caught a fish."

"No!"

"If it's a kiss, that won't surprise me."

I've been holding the bracelet in my hand while we've been talking, and she just notices.

"What's in your hand, mister?" she asks.

I held out my hand and open it, showing her the bracelet I was given.

"It's beautiful," she says. "Is it for me?"

"Yeah, " I say, "I want you to have it."

"Did you just find it in the water or something?"

"No, it fell out of a snowflake."

"A snowflake? You need to go easy on the pot."

Even though I forgot I had it until now, I say, "I just want to give you a remembrance of me, and this seems like the right time."

"Oh, you mean after that thing you did?"

"The thing I did?"

"I mean that thing I did to you?"

"No, not because of that. More like now that you're hanging out with me, you're like a friend, a companion, a . . ."

"Lover?" she finishes my sentence. "Well, I love it."

She slips it on and admires it for a few seconds, turning her wrist one-way and then the other. She gets close to me and whispers, "I really love it." She puts her arms around my neck and kisses me very softly. Then she whispers, "Thank you."

We head back towards the concert area, but when we get to the fence behind the stage, I can see John Sebastian. He's just finished his set and is talking with some friends. We start jumping up and down calling loudly, "JOHN! JOHN!" We are really just pretending to be groupies, but we get his attention, and he waves his friends on and heads towards us.

We shake fingers through the link, and of course, we tell him he was great even though we hadn't heard his whole set, and Gail doesn't even know who he is.

"I didn't even know you were gonna be here," I say.

"Either did I," he answers. "I happened to be at the airport and noticed my old road manager down on the runway, so I ran down to him and told him I wanted to get to Woodstock.

He told me the only way I was gonna get here was to hop into his helicopter right now with The Incredible String Band because the road to this place is impossible to get through."

"Wow! Lucky timing," I say.

"So I got in, and we took off. As we flew, I saw buses, cars and tents everywhere, long before I could see the crowd of people at the stage. Man, it was far-out. After we landed, and I got more familiar with the surroundings, I noticed the weather was really bad for the instruments and suggested to Chip that we should have a tent to keep all the instruments in. He agreed with my concern and put me in charge."

"So," Gail asks, "I guess they gave you a chance to play?"

"Not exactly, but today the stage was so wet and dangerous for the equipment and the amplifiers, they needed someone who can hold the attention of the audience with one non-electric guitar while standing in front of one lone microphone. So they said to me, 'John, you're here, and we've elected you to play the acoustic guitar.' I was handed Tim Hardin's guitar, and I took to the stage as they continued sweeping off the water. So I got to be here, and also got to enjoy performing here as well."

"You were excellent, man," I say.

At this point, he realizes he has to leave, so we say our goodbyes.

Sebastian's name is on the Woodstock Memorial Plaque, but it's the only misspelled name, (spelled Sabastian). There were decision makers that wanted it changed, but it was just too costly to do over, but it's kind of ironic, since he wasn't supposed to be at Woodstock anyway.

124

CHAPTER 17: Breathing

We continue walking around the fenced area to a more open field and there are many open areas around for people to gather, but in this particular area there are almost 100 people that have migrated to participate in a yoga class. We hear the yoga instructor say,

> "Now very slowly bring yourself back up. Lower your legs, and bring yourself back up. Now breathe as fast as you can."

There is a guy on a platform, and everyone on the grass is facing in his direction listening, and doing what he says. We learn he is actually from the Hog Farm.

He continues,

> "Yoga means union. It's the same as using drugs, but it gives you a force, a rush, same channel that drugs do for you, but this way, you can do it yourself. You don't have to score, it's in you, and all you need is clean air. I'm from California, and there are only a few months of that."

"You're not kidding?" I say, just loud enough for some others to hear me.

He continues,

> "Man has experimented with it for at least 6,000 years and gotten very high with it."

"I don't really have that much time," I say, trying to be funny in my own way. Gail laughs, and so do some of the others who can hear me.

He explains that,

> "The nerve impulses can pass in harmony through the spinal cord and put you in a state of suspended sensation."

"Let's try it," Gail suggests.

"You're kidding me, right?"

She sits down and pulls me down next to her.

He continues,

> "Lie down again. Start breathing in and out, in and out, with a steady rhythm. In . . . out, now breathe faster, feeling the energy growing, now, in out, in out, in out."

Gail lies down, but I'm still sitting up and watching everyone else. Their bodies are jerking and convulsing like fish out of water. Then Gail pulls on me to lie on top of her, which I gladly do.

I know that lying on top of her is not part of the yoga exercise, but as I do it, she put her arms around me and pulls me down on top. After about five seconds she whispers in my ear, "I don't think this is part of the breathing exercise . . . since I can hardly breathe." I quickly lift myself up and roll onto my back right next to her. My hand lies on top of her hand, and as her fingers separate, mine fall in place, filling the void. For the first time, our hands clasp. It may sound ridiculous, but I feel closer to her now than when she got me off during Santana. I give her hand a little squeeze, and she reciprocates.

I stay at her side, holding her hand, and resting my eyes. I can still hear the others breathing heavily around us, but I'm breathing heavily inside.

"Oh look," I hear her say and open my eyes.

Up in the sky is a plane – skywriting. White smoke emits from the back as it completes a perfect circle and is looping around without drawing anything, but as it passes through the circle, the writing starts again, and he cut that circle in half with a straight line right through it.

I whisper, "That's like us, two halves that equal a whole." I can feel her squeeze my hand again. Then the plane makes another smokeless loop and adds a line from the circle to the straight line and loops around one last time adding another line, making the biggest peace sign I have ever seen. It's fantastic. We watch it, lying still on the ground while everyone else is doing the breathing exercises. The peace sign starts to slowly dissipate as the whole thing moves further across the sky and eventually away.

"Free your body," the yoga teacher says.

I've done enough heavy breathing, which is actually none at all. We get up and walk away, still holding hands. Further on are a couple smoking a joint and motion to us to join them.

We sit down and share introductions.

"Jim," "Gail," "Bonnie," "Glenn."

"You look like such a nice couple," Bonnie says.

"Well that's nice of you to say since we just met over there." I point to the yoga area.

"Really?" she acts surprised.

Before I can say I'm kidding, Gail butts in, "Yes, I really like the way he breathes."

Jim finishes his hit on the joint and passes it to Gail. Then he lets out a huge puff of smoke and says, "You guys didn't just meet."

Bonnie looks confused.

"Yes, you're right," Gail answers. "We didn't just meet now, but we did a few days ago."

I look at Gail.

"Only two days ago. Wow! But it sure seems a lot longer," I say to Gail.

"Yes," Gail says. "Three days." We all laugh.

"We just got here this morning," Jim says. "We must have walked 100 miles."

"He's exaggerating," Bonnie informs us.

"You think?" Jim questions. "All I know is it was far."

"Let me ask you guys something," Bonnie says looking at us, specifically me. "I want to know what you think. Jim loves the Canned Heat and wants to jump up on the stage with them when they play."

"Yeah?" I ask.

"Well, doesn't that sound crazy?"

Gail looks at me. "I'll take this one." Then turns to Bonnie and proceeds to respond, "You should support your man in anything he wants to do."

128

Man, she just keeps getting better, I think to myself.

Bonnie is stunned, and Jim says, "Right on!"

Bonnie a little disappointed by Gail's answer and looks back at me.

"What do you think, Glenn?"

"First, he'll probably never even get that close to the stage. Second, if he does, he'll never get up onto the stage, and third, if he does . . . I think it'd be cool."

We all laugh again, except for Bonnie. Jim offers me a cigarette, and I tell him I don't smoke. Then Jim offers the open pack to Gail who doesn't take one either.

At this point we are getting a little hungry, either because it's dinnertime or because of the pot. Either way, we decide to go back to the campsite again. On the way we can find out who is entertaining the crowd now. We find out we missed Keef Hartley Band, but I don't care. I learned they were the first British group to play Woodstock, and this was their first appearance in the United States.

Now The Incredible String Band is playing because they had refused to play in the rain last night. It would've been better for them to play yesterday because it was folk music night, and they're a psychedelic folk rock band. Today we all want to hear rock music.

The clouds are rolling in, blocking the sun. The overcast coupled with this music seem to be putting many to sleep right now, but we're listening to the music as we walk and it slowly fades away as we leave The Bowl and walk along side the cornfield to our campsite.

CHAPTER 18: Janis

We get to the campsite, and Gail looks into my eyes as she snuggles up closer. She leans her head towards my ear, and in a hushed voice whispers, "Do you have any munchies?" Then she backs away, waiting for my answer.

"Why do you do that?"

"Do what?"

"You know what you just did?" I ask.

"What?"

"You get real sexy, like in the pond, then you splashed me and ran off. Now you get real close and sound sexy again and then change the subject to munchies, which is not sexy at all."

"You don't think munchies are sexy?"

"Well, not really. Besides, all I brought is good protein food, like eggs, peanut butter, the beans I gave away, cheese, and I don't remember the point I was trying to make because you're so damn pretty to look at, I can't remember what I'm complaining about."

"Oh, Glenn, I'm just teasing you," she says, as a smile comes across her face. "I'll try not to do that anymore."

Then she gives me a quick kiss on the cheek and walks towards her tent.

Looking back at me she says,

"You'll miss it when I stop though. Now get some cheese ready, and I'll bring dessert."

I go searching for the cheese and crackers. When she doesn't come out, I step by her tent and yell that I'm gonna fill up the canteen.

"Okay!"

When I get back, she's sitting on the log and has changed into jeans with a very colorful sweater, with thick and thin stripes over an orange blouse with a simple peace sign in the center.

"You change your clothes a lot," I say.

"Well, once the sun goes down, it'll be chilly."

It's after six o'clock, and I go into the tent, put on a jacket myself, and grab the cheese and crackers. As we eat, she informs me that she plans to stay with me tonight to watch the concert. I tell her that's great, and that we can keep each other warm. She nods in agreement and then softly kisses my cheek and then brushes it.

"Oh, did I have crumbs on my face?" I ask.

"No!" she says laughing.

"Then what are you rubbing off?"

"Nothing, it's my kiss, I'm rubbing in."

"Where's the dessert you were bringing?"

"It's in my tent, I'll go get it now."

She comes back with a large brownie and a large glass of milk.

Jokingly I ask, "Where's your dessert?"

She shoots back, "We're sharing, You Silly."

When we finish, we head to the arena to listen to the music. It's not dark yet, but I want us to be on the blanket by the time the sun disappears. Tonight I just want to relax with her and listen to the music since we hadn't heard many groups all day. As we enter the field, we hear,

"Ladies and gentleman, to continue, it's our delight to present Canned Heat!"

"Hey!" Bob Hite screams into the microphone. "We're just gonna play a little blues."

The harmonica wails a few notes, and the band joins in. It sounds great, and then the lyrics fill our ears,

"I find that love is really good to me
I find that love is something good to me
You see a man can love a woman
So together they can be free"

We're walking slowly down the slight slope toward our seats and I ask out loud, "Who was on before Canned Heat?" Someone responds with The Incredible String Band, so I tell Gail we didn't miss anybody while we were at the campsite, unless you want to count The Incredible String Band. We get to our blanket. That's right, "our blanket," and she sits down. Just before I sit I glance over in Sharon's direction and see other people sitting there. She's gone back to camp I concluded. Then I sit between Brian on my left and Gail to my right.

Brian whispers, "You look like you had a good time earlier," quickly nodding his head towards Gail. I should be embarrassed, but instead, I'm proud. I answer Brian with a big smile.

Let me just say, what Gail did to me never happened in quite that way before. In fact, someone like Gail never happened to me in any way before. There's no doubt I really like her, and I'm pretty confident she likes me.

The song ends and their lead singer thanks the crowd and continues,

> "Ahh! You're really good tonight. You know this is the most outrageous spectacle I have ever witnessed, ever. There's only one thing I wish . . . I sure got to pee, and there sure ain't nowhere to go."

By now it's around 7:30 p.m., and evening is upon us. The sky is light blue, while the sun's shining its last rays for the day. Above us are dark blue dense clouds. The spotlights from the towers are casting down on a lone guitarist with a hollowing voice and a harmonica sound backing up his words. The song is subtle and sweet, and then the tempo becomes pronounced, and the vocalist goes, "1, 2, 3, 4." They break into "Going Up the Country," and it's glorious.

Sam starts to hand me a joint, but Gail grabs my hand and says,

> "Not now. Not tonight."

> I blurt out, "Let's just say, not yet,"

Then we watch Canned Heat jamming away on stage. Then someone jumps on the stage. I remember seeing the guy next to us with binoculars early on, so I turn to him and ask if I can borrow them. Our seats are very good for watching the concert, but I want to take a real good look to confirm who I think jumped on stage.

133

"Gail!" I say with a laugh. "That's Jim."

"Who's Jim?" she asks.

"Jim! Remember Jim and Bonnie? Well, that's Jim up there with Bob from Canned Heat. They'll probably throw him off the stage in a minute."

"YOU GET HIM, JIM!" she screams.

Now she grabs the binoculars to take a look for herself.

"That looks like Jim alright, but they're not throwing him off the stage, he's busy lighting up a smoke."

"Let me see. He's with the lead singer, Bob Hite, and Bob's holding onto Jim like he's his best friend."

"He's Jim's new buddy." she adds.

We start laughing, and I hand the binoculars back, thanking the guy. I'm starting to feel real high now, probably from the excitement. I'm glad I didn't take that hit from Sam. Then I wonder,

"Gail, was there something in that brown — "

She quickly lunges forward, holding my arms at my side and starts kissing me to keep me from finishing the sentence. When she stops, I can't remember what I was asking. I just lie there with her on top of me. I don't even try to get up, but I'm so relaxed and having her so close is comforting. Then I remember my accusation, and in a whisper I ask, "There was something in that brownie, wasn't there?"

"Yes," she replies, "and I'm sure you'll like it."

I'm on my back, and there's no sense trying to get up, with her on top of me, I couldn't be happier.

For the next six hours, I'm in a state of euphoria. Gail is right there with me. She assures me it's not acid or anything like that, just plain old marijuana in the form of a brownie.

Then I hear,

> "Ladies and Gentlemen, to continue, please greet Mountain!"

We're very stoned, and somewhere in their set, I hear Leslie West, their lead guitarist, speak,

> "Felix is gonna sing a song written by Jack Bruce, who I'm sure you heard of called 'Theme From An Imaginary Western.'"

It's a beautiful song, and I'm just sort of floating to it without leaving my seat. It's a very peaceful song even though Mountain usually plays rock. Jack Bruce was a member of Cream with Eric Clapton and Ginger Baker.

Gail and I are just laying beside each other, still taking in the sound of the rock band. I can feel Gail's warmth as she leans against me, kissing me occasionally, but mostly when it's quiet between the groups. I guess she feels like she has to do something during the silence, but it's not a make-out sessions, just a kiss usually on the cheek, a hug, or a squeeze.

"You are the cutest girl at this concert," I whisper to her.

"You're being funny again."

"You know, I'm really starting to — "

There she goes again putting her mouth on mine. I know she's kissing me in order to stop me from finishing my sentence, but how does she know what I'm gonna say. What if I was gonna say, "You know I'm really starting to . . . have an itch on my ass." Really how does she know?

Then we hear loud and clear,

> "One of the best fucking rock groups in the world, The Grateful Dead!"

Their music captivates the audience, and we, like many Dead Heads, sit up and begin swaying to the music. During the next few songs, Gail sits in my lap as I hold her. Canned Heat and Mountain had played for about an hour each, but the Grateful Dead is going on an hour and a half already. Suddenly during "Turn on Your Love Light," the lights go out on stage, and the song ends abruptly. It's because the amplifiers got overloaded, and the electricity cut off. That ends their set, but within 30 minutes, the music begins again.

It's now after midnight into Sunday morning, but to us it's still Saturday night. The groups continue to play their music with relatively short breaks in-between. They will play all night until the sun peeks out over the land declaring it a new day.

> "Ladies and gentleman, please welcome the Creedence Clearwater Revival!"

If the group's name isn't heard, it's still quite clear who is taking the stage by the very familiar guitar riff from "Born on the Bayou." Everyone knows its Creedence. Gail and I are really digging them, and we are either singing together or singing at each other because we both know so many of their songs.

Creedence was the first major group to sign with Woodstock Ventures and that helped bring credibility to the whole concert, which encouraged many of the other artists to sign on. John Fogerty, later said about his time on stage, "It was about 12:30 a.m., and it looked like everyone was asleep, but I will never forget this one guy on the other end of the darkness about a quarter mile away on the far end of The Bowl, flicking his Bic lighter. That night I played the show for that guy."

They leave the stage almost an hour later, and Gail and I are still enjoying the high from her brownie. Once again, the silence between acts makes her a little frisky. How did I get to be so lucky? It's because I'm such a lovable guy, I guess. It's either really late at night or very early in the morning when the silence on stage is broken again by,

"Please welcome with us, Miss Janis Joplin!"

Gail immediately stops leaning on me and stands up as Janis comes out on the platform. The woman that sings the blues comes out appropriately dressed in blue. She has on blue decorated bell-bottoms with a blue blouse and a flyaway blue jacket with wide sleeves like what a mystical sorcerer would wear. Then she proceeds to cast a spell on all of us through her performance at 2:00 a.m. I sit watching Gail swaying, dancing, and even doing weird movement in unison to the rhythmic sound of Janis for the next hour. Janis's raspy voice sings out her rendition of the Bee Gees' "To Love Somebody." Between songs, the girl that will later be known as "Pearl" addresses the audience:

> "How are you out there? Everybody okay? You staying stoned and have enough water and a place to sleep? Because, ya know . . . I don't mean to be preachy, but we ought to remember music's for grooving, man, and not for putting yourself through bad changes. You don't have to take anybody's shit just to like music, man."

Then her echoing voice thrills the spectators as she does, "Try (Just a Little Bit Harder)," while a red light is casting down on her, and she looks like a little flame of light. She ends with "Piece of My Heart," and it looks like she's done, but she comes back to play one more song. Gail is still clapping for Janis minutes after she leaves the stage. I just stand up behind her to hold her, and she spins around and slumps in my arms as she goes limp from exhaustion. She has 30 minutes to relax and refuel until the next act is on.

By the way, Janis Joplin dies on October 4, 1970, a little over a year after Woodstock. Several people died that week from the same batch of heroin that was more potent than normal. It seemed the dealer's druggist was out of town, so he cut the heroin himself. Not very well it would seem.

August 17, 1969 (Sunday)
CHAPTER 19: The Who

"Ladies and gentleman, Sly and the Family Stones!"

Right away their funky beat has the whole place rocking, but during their big hit, Sly has everyone on their feet as he dances wildly on stage and sings out, "I wanna take you higher!" To which everyone raises their hands and echoes his call, "HIGHER!" Every time he sings out that word the audience sings back, "HIGHER!" There's no denying that this crowd is fully awake at 4:00 a.m.

Once they leave the stage, we feel much less stoned from the brownie, so we take two hits apiece from a joint Sam lights up. I notice Gail borrowing the binoculars again to look at the stage to see who's setting up for the next powerful performance.

Gail hands back the binoculars and stands, takes my hand, and pulls me up off the blanket.

"What's up?" I ask.

"Let's get closer," she says.

"Okay, but the crowd is gonna make it hard to get up close. I think you're very, very beautiful and I would let you through, but I don't think you're gonna get very far."

"Just leave it to me," she response.

We move up further than I expect because when people are standing, there's more space between them, but we still aren't getting very close. Gail is determined to venture onward. It's dark, but I can see the silhouettes of the hippies' heads, and there are also a lot of lit joints glowing like lightning bugs in the night. When I think we reach a dead end, a complete stand still, she yanks my hand and continues forward and starts shouting,

"GLENN! GLENN!" as she moves onward.

We start to get a little momentum as we keep moving forward and closer to the stage.

"GLENN! GLENN!" she cries out again.

She keeps yelling Glenn, and I'm keeping the pace, so there's no need to yank me anymore. The crowd is opening up like the Red Sea as she continues yelling my name in search of me. We finally get as far as we can, which is two rows from the front. At this point she spins around and puts her arms around my neck and kisses me. Now I can see what she had seen through the binoculars. On the stage, written on the bass drum is "The Who." She remembered the one group I really wanted to see. Then she stands back looking at me. I can see her face somewhat in the dark, she's looking right at me, and I hear her ask,

"So you think I'm very, very beautiful?"

"If I said it . . . then I meant it."

"Ladies and Gentlemen, would you please show your appreciation, they came to us especially for this show, please warmly welcome The Who!"

The beam of light that lit up the stage as we watched from afar is now a very bright beam of light coming down from right above us, casting a spotlight onto the platform. I gently turn Gail around as The Who takes the stage.

140

Pete Townshend is in all white, while Roger Daltrey comes out bare-chested with a beige sleeved vest with long white fringe hanging down from each arm. Strangely enough, their first song is "Heaven and Hell," a song I'm less familiar with, but it doesn't matter because what I'm familiar with is Daltrey holding onto the microphone cord and spinning it 10 or so feet away and pulling it back and catching it in his hand. Townshend also has his electrifying classic move of playing his guitar in a motion like a windmill, stretching out his arm, bringing it around, and hitting the strings.

My arms drape around Gail as she stands in front of me with The Who right before our very eyes. After their next song, "I Can't Explain," they go into songs from *Tommy*. *Tommy* has just been released in May of this year, and it seems like everyone knows the words to at least "Pinball Wizard." The crowd is going wild.

What happens after that song is just a very strange occurrence. We probably wouldn't even be aware of it if we weren't so damn close. I learn from the hippie sitting next to us, the person that appears on stage right after that song is Abbie Hoffman. He goes straight to the microphone:

> "I think this is a pile of shit while John Sinclair rots in prison!" he shouts.

> Pete Townshend steps in and screams, "FUCK OFF!"

It looks like Hoffman is gonna say something else, but Townshend strikes him in the head with his guitar and yells,

> "FUCK OFF MY FUCKIN' STAGE!" and at that point, Hoffman leaves.

"What the hell was that all about?" Gail asks.

"I don't know."

The band continues with "Do You Think It's Alright." Nearly two hours later, the band explodes into "My Generation," while we, the audience, go into a frenzy. From that song, they go straight into their final song, "Naked Eye," and Townshend starts banging his guitar onto the stage causing screeching feedback over the speakers. He jumps up and lands down on his knees as the base of his guitar is driven into the hard wooden floor of the stage. He does that a few more times as his guitar splinters, and then he lays it down by a speaker and walks away, but turns around and comes back, picks up the guitar, takes a few steps forward and tosses it out into the audience right next to us. The guy who told me about Hoffman catches it. Wow! The crowd bursts into applause as The Who leaves the stage, and the lights go out.

Gail and I are delighted by the performance. We head back to our blanket, moving between the crowds that Gail had outwitted earlier. I see people starting to sit back down or lay down to go to sleep. Thanks to our little flag, we are lucky enough to find our blanket since Brian and Sam are gone. We lay down, and she pulls my arm over her body so we are spooning. I place my hand onto her breast and I just hold her close as we fall asleep.

A couple hours later, the sun is shining across the field, and the music begins again starting with a drum and a little warm up of the other instruments. Then I hear a voice I recognize as Grace Slick,

> "Alright, friends, you have seen the heavy groups, now you will see morning maniac music, believe me, yeah . . . It's a new dawn."

As the band starts playing "Somebody To Love," Grace yells out, "MORNING PEOPLE!" and goes into the song. I'm still holding Gail, and the lyrics from the song fill my head,

"Don't you want somebody to love?
Don't you need somebody to love?
Wouldn't you love somebody to love?
You better find somebody to love."

Various songs fill my ears as I drift in and out of sleep. "Wooden Ships," "Volunteers," and "White Rabbit." Then all I hear is silence.

CHAPTER 20:
Breakfast in Bed for 400,000

Our sleep is broken when a raspy voice comes over the microphone announcing,

> "Good morning. What we have in mind is breakfast in bed for 400,000. Now, it's not gonna be steak and eggs or anything, but it's gonna be good food, and we're gonna get it to you. It's not just the Hog Farm either; it's like the Ohio Mountain Family and the Pranksters and everybody else that are volunteering, putting in their time into the free kitchen. In fact it's everybody; we're all feeding each other. WE MUST BE IN HEAVEN, MAN! There is always a little bit of heaven in a disaster area."

We look at each other and start pointing to the stage as we say in unison, "That's Hugh," and we both start laughing. Next Hugh says, "Okay, here it comes, mess call." Then a bugler player toots out a very poor rendition of "Mess Call," over the speakers.

When that finishes, I give Gail a quick kiss on the lips and say, "Good Morning." I stand up and stretch, and once she stands up to also stretch we notice that there are volunteers at the stage passing out food to the audience sitting in front. We learn that a truck has driven behind the stage so they can feed the people in front, that haven't really left often for food. Lisa Law, the woman who took my can of beans from Hugh, is helping with others from the Hog Farm and the other families that Hugh mentioned. They're handing out cups of granola.

Many people might think that Wavy Gravy is here at Woodstock, but the truth is he isn't here. Well, let me explain. The kind guy with the kazoo that I've run into several times is Hugh Romney, but it turns out, he later becomes Wavy Gravy, but he doesn't get the name for another two weeks at the Texas International Pop Festival. The story goes that he's exhausted from helping out at that festival and is lying onstage when B.B. King is to be the next performer. As Hugh started to get up, B.B. King puts his hand on Hugh's shoulder and asks, "Are you Wavy Gravy?" Romney replied, "Yes." B.B. says, "It's okay; I can work around you." B.B. King and Johnny Winter jammed for hours, and Romney believed this was a mystical event and changed his name legally to Wavy Gravy, but at Woodstock, he's still my favorite guy, Hugh Romney.

The speakers start to hum, and a new voice is heard in the air,

"Okay, people, we have a *New York Times*. On the front page, we have on the left a great big aerial photo of a huge mass of people which are you. And it says, 'Music wasn't magic for hippies at Woodstock Music and Art Fair. 300,000 at Folk Rock Fair camp out in a sea of mud. Bethel, New York, August 16th. Despite massive traffic jams, drenching thunderstorms, shortage of food, water, and medical facilities, about 300,000 young people swarmed over this rural area. With the prospect of drugs and the excitement of making this scene, campers came in groves, camping in the woods, laughing in the mud, smoking, talking and listening to music. Participants were well behaved according to both the sponsors and police even though about 75 persons in the area got busted for narcotics. There's a shortage of water, and cars are backed up for twenty miles.'

All in all, it says you've been pretty groovy, man. I want to thank you for being beautiful, man. You're really making the show."

Gail acknowledges that the news report is pretty cool and that we should head back to the campsite, but stop in the cornfield first. Upon arriving at her tent, we notice the bearded guy's not here, so I go inside the tent with her. She opens the sleeping bag so it's like a double bed size so we can both lie down. She takes her blouse off, but doesn't face me, and I take off my shirt. She pulls a blanket over us, and we spoon again, this time I can feel the warmth from her bare back against my bare chest. She takes my hand and pulls it over her body, but this time she puts it onto her bare breast, and I can feel it pressing against my palm. I'm holding her, and she feels amazing under my arm. "You're making this weekend fantastic," I whisper. She doesn't respond, so I figure she's asleep.

I wake up first, and it can't be more than an hour and a half later. I slip out from under the blanket and stand up as not to disturb her. I back out of the tent and close the flap. I can see the flap to my tent is closed, so I know Brian and Sam are gone because when we are sleeping, we always leave it half open so as to get fresh air. The sun is shining through white clouds directly above me, so I figure it's around noontime. The concert is supposed to start at 2:00 p.m. today, so I still have time to grab something to eat. I go back to my tent and notice the smell of coffee and a couple sitting on my favorite log holding cups.

I enter my tent and change clothes. I put on a fresh pair of jeans, a T-shirt, my bandana and my sneakers. I head back to Gail's tent where I left her sleeping and I open the flap, and step inside. She's lying on her back, blanket covering her up to her jeans, and she appears to be sleeping. The sun's light shining on the tent's canvas is casting an orange hue throughout the inside of the tent. Her long brown hair is flowing over her shoulders covering both her breasts. "You look lovely," I whisper under my breath. She's so exposed and yet so covered up. The curvature under her breasts can be seen coming out from under her hair, but her nipples are completely covered.

146

"You're up, aren't you?" I whisper.

No answer and no movement.

"You're up," I say louder.

I can see her lips slightly curl up at both sides of her mouth as she starts smiling.

"You're up!" I say again.

"Of course I'm up, You Silly."

"You are such a tease," I say.

"No. Really I'm not."

"Yeah," I say, "really you are. You said you would stop doing that."

"I did. You just caught me sleeping."

"Yeah! And your hair fell in just the right places to cover you up. That's how I knew you weren't asleep."

"What's for breakfast?" she asks.

"It's lunchtime, but I can still make you eggs."

"Do you have bacon?"

"No, but I have a sausage."

"That I already know," she says winking at me. "Can you please make me breakfast while I get dressed?"

"Sure, but only if I can watch . . . I mean wait for you."

"Breakfast, please. Now get out of here!"

After about twenty minutes pass, I shout,

"GAIL! THE FOODS ALMOST READY."

"I AM TOO!" she yells back.

Another couple of minutes, and she comes out wearing her tight jean shorts and a white blouse, but she also has on my bracelet. I tell her she looks lovely.

"You said that earlier," she tells me.

"Yeah, but I thought you were asleep. It was true then, and it's true now, you do look lovely."

"Got to go to the little girl's field."

She scampers off quickly, either knowing her food is almost ready or because she really has to go badly. When she returns, the log, our log, is vacant, so we sit down and eat. We decide to go right to the concert area when we're done. She gets a joint while I clean the pan and refill the canteen. We sit on the grass giving some other campers the log and give them a few hits as well. Then we head out.

CHAPTER 21:
Max Yasgur and Joe Cocker

We walk toward the arena, get past the cornfield and stop to look down at the stage together as we did the first night. At that time, it was almost a completely empty field with lights flashing and sparks flying as the stage was being erected. Today, the field is far from empty, with 400,000 people, according to Hugh, enjoying peace, love, and music on a field owned by a simple farmer named Max Yasgur.

The stage is abuzz, even though no one is particularly performing right now. It's an incredible stage where the artists have performed and will continue to perform in front of the largest gathering of people to date; much bigger than anybody could have ever possibly imagined. The stage amplifies the sounds of my generation, through the music, that brought us all here. The stage, where the Gods of the music industry can each tell their story, actually our story, through their songs. I know it all sounds a bit cliché, but that doesn't make it any less true.

Gail and I stop and peer out at the crowd. I'm holding her from behind with my arms around her waist as she leans her head backward onto me, and we look in awe at this unbelievable sight.

"Did you ever expect anything like this?" she asks.

"No, not even in my wildest dreams."

"There's never been anything like this."

"You're right," I say, "this is something special; this might change the world."

"Don't get so carried away," she laughs. "A year from now you won't even remember it."

"I don't think I'll ever forget it."

Then I turn her around to face me.

"There's no way I'm gonna forget this weekend because there's no way I'm gonna forget you. You are a very big part of why this weekend is so unforgettable. I think, I — "

"Stop right there!" she interrupts, putting her hand on my mouth to stop me as usual.

Then she puts her arms around me and squeezes. She brings her lips to mine and proceeds to kiss me, softly and sweetly. Obviously, she doesn't want to hear my loving words. Her tongue tries to inch its way between my lips, but my lips stay firmly closed putting up a resistance. I'm a little annoyed by her attitude. I'm trying hard to stop her advancing tongue because I'm a little angry. She's so sweet, really, and so much fun and I'll be damned, I can't help but give in, and our tongues wrestle for just enough time to forgive. When she stops and steps back, my eyes are still closed savoring the lasting kiss, and I can feel my body sway just a bit. Then she whacks me in the arm, and says,

"Can we go now?"

She proceeds to lead the way towards the blanket, but looks back a couple of times to make sure I'm okay. Please don't have any doubt I'm fine.

Brian and Sam are there when we get to our turf. We discuss what an amazing event this is turning out to be and how many of the groups put on exceptional performances. We came prepared with food and the appropriate drugs. I guess it's safe to say that now, and we never once felt like this place is a disaster area.

I've been to the pond and anywhere else I wanted to go. Gail has also. We never needed to call anybody, and we slept on the field or in our own tents. We even have our own bathroom and water fountain. It's fantastic. I can't imagine anything can put a damper on this wonderful weekend festival, but something can and something will.

Chip, breaks the silence,

> "We have a gentleman with us. It's the gentleman whose farm we are on, Mr. Max Yasgur."

I told Gail I had talked with him yesterday on my way to the Hog Farm. If I had any doubt that it was Mr. Yasgur, I have none now. He's still wearing a white button-down, short sleeve shirt, probably not the exact same one, but obviously that's his style, and it looks real good on him. He has on his dark rimmed glasses and holds up his hand flashing the peace sign.

> "Is this on?" he asks.

The crowd cheers and claps and then lets Mr. Yasgur continue,

> "I'm a farmer. I don't know how to speak to 20 people at one time, let alone a crowd like this. But I think you people have proven something to the world. This is the largest group of people ever assembled in one place. We had no idea that there would be this size group, and because of that, you've had quite a few inconveniences as far as water, food, and so forth. Your producers have done a mammoth job to see that you're taken care of. They'd enjoy a vote of thanks. But above that, the important thing that you've proven to the world is that a half a million kids, and I do call you kids because I have children that are older than you, a half a million young people can get together and have three days of fun and music and have nothing but fun and music, and I bless you for it!"

He's a beautiful man, Gail says, and I have to agree. It's Sunday, the last day of the concert, and it's almost time for today's show to begin and it does, as soon as Max leaves the stage.

"Ladies and gentleman, Joe Cocker!"

First just the band comes out and plays a couple of instrumentals. Then Joe Cocker comes out. He's a raspy, voiced singer who is not well known, but he takes to the microphone in his blue jeans and brown tie-dye shirt. His back-up band is The Grease Band, and they break into their first song, "Dear Landlord." His body moves like he's having convulsions, and his hands work independently from each other. His left hand appears to be playing the cords on a guitar while his right hand appears to be moving in a disjointed fashion trying to go around his back. His body rises up on and off his toes, but his harsh voice only helps him command the stage. He knocks out familiar songs, "Feelin' Alright," "Just Like a Woman," and "I Shall Be Released." Then he introduces his final song,

> "We're gonna leave you with a usual thing, all I can say, as I've said to many people, this title just about puts things in focus. It's called 'With A Little Help From My Friends.' Remember us."

It starts with the organ, drums follow, and the rest of the instruments join in, and then he belts out the best damn rendition of a Beatles song I've ever heard. I don't believe anyone has ever done a Beatle song better than the Beatles themselves except for this performance by Joe Cocker, live at Woodstock. He's one of the most unusual performer that I've ever seen, with his odd movements, his body twitching, hair waving as his head bobbles back and forth, his right foot pointing inward towards his left making him look awkward, yet none of that stops him from singing perfectly. His raspy voice only enhances the song and the members of his band are excellent at backing him up. It's incredible to the end. It's his last song, and he leaves the stage with applause until he's out of sight.

It was this performance that skyrocketed him to fame, but not so much from the Woodstock crowd, but by the millions that watch him in the film, "Woodstock" that came out several months later.

CHAPTER 22:
No Rain, No Rain, No Rain

It's just after 3 p.m. when Joe Cocker leaves the stage. I turn to Gail, but she isn't looking at me; she's actually looking past me into the sky. I see her lose her smile as the blood rushes from her cheeks, and her face is turning pale. I turn around and see the backs of Brian and Sam as they run up the slope towards the campsite. Then, I see the sky. Above our heads, it's still bright and clear, while in the distance looms a horrible darkness that is eating up the light as it heads our way. I can see the heavy flow of rain falling directly below the darkness as it's closing in on us.

"Should we leave?" she asks in a panic. "Should we get out of here?"

There's no question there's fear in her voice, and I don't know how to answer. I turn back to her, and stutter, trying to answer correctly, "I, I think — "

Suddenly a voice comes over the speakers:

"Looks like we're going to get a little bit of rain, so you better cover up, if it does. If we should lose power, just move it out, but we'll sit here with you. It'll be okay."

We can hear the chattering of the crowd, and the wind is picking up. We can hear the thunder rumbling, and the stage crew is scrambling about trying to tie things down. It looks like everyone in the audience is standing. We can see some people trying to hold the plastic sheets over their heads in anticipation of the heavy rain, but the wind is filling them like sails making them uncontrollable and whipping them out of the hands of some of the people.

154

Then we hear the voice again,

> "Please get down from the towers." Chip demands.
> "Everybody just sit down and wrap yourself up, we're
> going to have to ride it out. Hold on to your neighbor,
> man. Please get off the towers; we don't need any extra
> weight on them. Also move away from the towers, the
> spotlight might give us some problems. Everybody that's
> in the back, please move further back. Please move back.
> We have to get away from these towers."

The thunder has gotten louder and more frequent. Most people
are standing, but many have decided to sit and are covering
themselves up in little groups, and I can see the blankets that were
under them are now over them like umbrellas. Little mounds in
various colors can be seen across the field. The people standing
are wrapping themselves in their blankets trying to keep dry, while
others without blankets can't do anything to protect themselves
against the rain.

We are standing, and I'm holding Gail to comfort her as we look
at the sky, which is turning a dark gray right above our heads. It
seemed far away before the first announcement, but is swiftly
approaching us. We'll be okay I tell her, even though I'm not sure
myself. We wrap ourselves up in the blanket and cover the blanket
with a plastic sheet. We look out at the crowd. This raging storm
with its sudden winds and heavy rain is upon us. The rain falls
quickly and hard, and it's very noisy. Lightning is immediately
followed by a violent sound of thunder crashing down on us,
threatening the whole festival.

> "Please move away from the towers," he says again.

We can see most of the people are down from the towers, but a
few are still on them moving down very slowly.

"Cover up the equipment," we hear over the speakers.

He's talking to the workers on the stage, but the microphone is still on. We could see the trouble they're having with the tarps because of the wind.

> "Please move away from the towers. The wind is blowing this way, please stay on the other side of the towers. Just take it calm and easy, but move away from the towers."

We can hear screams from the crowds and can see the silhouettes of the people exiting the concert area, trying to find shelter elsewhere, but if they don't have tents or their cars aren't nearby, there is nowhere to hide. I think to myself, we must definitely stay away from trees, as another bright light streaks across the sky followed immediately by a burst of thunder. We are standing, but get knocked down by the wind; we quickly roll over and sit up clutching each other, with our faces touching cheek-to-cheek, peering out of our blanket. The light is now completely blotted out as the rain continues. The guy next to us is putting his clothes back on from sun bathing, that's how quick this storm approached. I ask him why he's putting clothes on in the rain. He answers, "I'm into nudity, man, not pneumonia." Most of the people are standing their ground by sitting in their place. Then someone in an outfit of vibrant primary colors runs up to Chip and speak into the microphone,

> "Maybe if we think really hard we can stop the rain. NO RAIN! NO RAIN! NO RAIN!"

The crowd remaining on the field is eager to respond,

> "NO RAIN! NO RAIN! NO RAIN!"

There isn't anything dry. On the stage, the canvases that had protected the musicians from the drizzle and hard rain on Friday and from the hot sun Saturday and earlier today are loose and flapping in the wind. They were held in place by four ropes, but now only by one that stops it from flying away altogether. I can see the scaffolding towers swaying back and forth, and for the first time since the concert started, there is nobody on them. The wind is pulling the plastic sheet away from us. We're trying to hold on to it, but the wind pulls it away and pushes us over even though we are already on the ground. We sit up again, still in the blanket that's now getting wet and muddy as I hold Gail very tightly, but I can start to feel the dampness seeping through the blanket.

We see people running with their blankets dragging in the mud. A few hippies are completely naked carrying their dry clothes bundled in their plastic sheet. Within 10 minutes everybody is drenched, and some look like wet rats walking away as if defeated. Some guys are yelling that the government had seeded the clouds to make it rain, and why doesn't the media report that.

Chip reinforces the last message we heard,

> "Like Barry says, let's think hard to get rid of the rain. NO RAIN! NO RAIN! NO RAIN!"

The crowd starts chanting louder and longer than before,

> "NO RAIN! NO RAIN! NO RAIN!"

He continues,

> "It's going to blow through. Try keeping yourselves comfortable. We have to put the power off. We're going to have to cut the microphones for a minute, hang in there with us. God bless ya. And again, watch those towers!"

Most of the crowd is holding tight in their spots. The water is running downhill from the back of the field, and the ones that thought they're keeping out the rain from above are now having it seep under them from the streams of water flowing. The water is also carrying cigarette packs and other small garbage. The storm lets no one escape its wrath.

The dark gray sky above seems to have stopped moving and is lingering above The Bowl, not moving nearly as fast as it did when it came upon us. The people that are standing up from the wet ground are battling the wind that's trying to rip their small hope of protection away from them. At the very least, it's trying to knock them to the ground, like it did us. One girl in jeans and a bra is just standing there fighting back by raising her fists in defiance of the weather, while another simply holds her hands out and spins in circles of joy just welcoming it.

The announcements have ceased for the time being, but the towers are the most concerning thing about the whole storm because they're swaying, and the distance it would cover if they fell could cause a lot of injuries and worse. We are far from that distance and feel safe.

We are soaking wet and our feet are muddy. Our blanket isn't doing much to help us anymore. We threw it off, and the wind takes it only a short distance because it's so damn heavy now. People are still all over the field. Maybe we should have gone back to the tent, but who knows if it's still standing. The wind on the field is stronger since there's nothing to block it, so going to the tent might have been a better idea.

Finally, it looks like the rain and wind are slowing down a bit, and the lightning and thunder is moving on. The whole storm lasted several hours, but looks like it has subsided. We all got through okay, and everybody is sort of rejoicing, I can see hippies pushing others in the mud for fun, laughing and slipping to the ground as well, but there is no way I'm getting Gail muddy.

I turn towards Gail, my long hair and my bandana are both sopping wet, and I can see her nipples very clearly through the wet fabric as her breasts push firmly against her white blouse. It clings to her breasts causing a beautiful view even though she's covered. To my amazement, my concern, which I never had before is, how do I cover her up, so that other guys won't see them . . . her . . . this time I'm right, them. I know I'm selfish. Her wet hair hangs straggly down her back, and she doesn't notice her nakedness as she laughs and spins around in the rain with her arms out. Her short jeans are wet and water is dripping down her bare legs all the way to her moccasins. Then I did what I didn't want to do. I pick up two handfuls of mud and quickly grab her breasts and I really try hard not to enjoy it. She stands still with her hands on her hips, not laughing any more.

"What are you doing?" she asks. "If you want to cop a feel, I would let you."

"Oh, I . . . Really?"

"Really, You Silly," she replies, and starts spinning again.

"I'm sorry, but I don't know what I was thinking."

What I'm thinking is that I got away without her knowing I got a little jealous. She stops spinning, seems a little dizzy, and falls in my arms. I can feel the mud from her chest get squeezed against my chest, but I don't care.

There's still a slight drizzle, but nothing close to the pounding we all took for the last few hours. The "no rain" chant has changed to a rhythmic mantra, "Ohh, oh, oh, oh, ohh," and the crowd starts banging sticks together or clanging cans, while others are hitting bottles with sticks or just clapping their hands, but whatever they're doing, it seems very tribal in nature. Everyone is moving to the rhythm and repeating, "Ohh, oh, oh, oh, ohh." It's a celebration, a ceremony, and a victory over their enemy, which in this case was the wind, the rain, the thunder, and the lightning. The wind has stopped; the drizzling has stopped, and everyone's completely wet.

Chip is back on the stage with the microphone,

"We'll be back with Country Joe in a second, as soon as we get set up."

There's a crowd gathering at a section down the middle of the field, so we walk over to see what's going on. The crowd is watching other hippies running down the hill and sliding in the mud, some feet first and others head first. I have my arm around Gail as we watch. As each person finishes their slide, there are cheers. Soon another free spirit slides down the muddy slope trying to skid even further than the last one. Others are dancing in the mud to the beat of the tribesmen. It's a sight to behold, but it looks disgusting to be covered in mud from head to toe. I suggest to Gail we head back to our tents to clean up.

We head back to the campsite holding hands, there's no reason to walk in single file anymore. We don't need to avoid people or sidestep blankets that lie in our pathway, because they're soaking wet, rolled over, or awkwardly folded from the wind. We still have to avoid puddles, mud, and garbage. Garbage bags are empty because the wind has blown them open, spreading garbage everywhere. The field is full of things people brought that might have seemed important before, but aren't worth anything now. The rain has destroyed everything.

I can hear a distinct bongo in the background as the chanting, "Ohh, oh, oh, oh, ohh," continues. Then, a sudden change to the chant could be heard, "Peace! Peace! Peace!" I look back to the area, trying to see where we were. Everything is gone, no sign of our blanket on the ground, because we had abandoned it to the wind. Brian and Sam's blankets may still be there under a puddle of water or buried under the mud or hidden by garbage, but who could ever find them now. But wait! There's something still there that defied the devastating storm. It's our little stick with the little fabric on it standing strong and tall, still in place. Brian and Sam could actually come back here and find our little turf.

As I look back towards the mudslide, I can see many hippies covered in mud, from head to toe, and when they aren't moving they actually look like statues. Between the grayish-brown silhouettes are bits of color from the mud-less people. But the most colorful person is on stage, the one that started the chant. I recognize him now, it's Barry Melton from Country Joe and The Fish and he's throwing cans of beer from the stage to the crowd, and there still seems to be a mass of people close to the stage.

"Gail, It looks like everybody's still here."

"Yes, it's hard to believe."

"There's also something else hard to believe."

"What's that, Glenn?"

"This show ain't over."

As scary as this was for the hundreds of thousands here, on stage and off, there is one promoter, Joel Rosenman, in his office in New York City that is thinking he is going to be considered the biggest murderer of all time because he keeps imagining that 50 to a 100 concertgoers are going to die by electrocution some time during this rainy weekend, but especially during this storm, which dropped 5 inches of rainfall in 3 hours.

CHAPTER 23: Our Final Night

Gail continues walking as we get to the cornfield, but I stop and look back. Look at that mob of people, I think to myself. Then I hear,

> "Ladies and Gentlemen, please warmly welcome, Country Joe and the Fish!"

They take to the stage like a fish to water. I can't believe I just said that. The crowd is more than welcoming them after the rain. They are political protesters that use their musical skill to express their views, such as in the song, "I Feel Like I'm Fixin' to Die Rag," that Joe sang yesterday. It started out with the "Fish Cheer," but really didn't spell fish.

Gail's out of sight, but I catch up with her back at the campsite, and she's standing with Brian and Sam. As I get there I hear Brian telling her they got really wet before they made it back to the tent. I could see his hair is all stringy but combed straight down, while Sam's Afro is flat.

> "We dried off," Brian says, "once we got in the tent, and the canvas held up very well against the wind."

> Gail says, "It looks like my tent did well too,"

> "One thunder clap," Sam adds, "was so loud and close I fell over inside the tent."

> "Yeah, that was funny," Brian says.

So they have changed and except for their hair they look fine. We, on the other hand, are drenched.

"I'm gonna dry off and clean up," she says. "Why don't you do the same and then come into my tent."

"That's exactly what I'm thinking,"

We move in opposite directions and leave Brian and Sam standing there.

"Hey, Sam," I shout, "Country Joe and the Fish are on." I told him because I know he is a big fan of CJ and the Fish.

"Cool," he says, and they head off to the field.

I'm cleaning off the mud with a towel outside my tent when I notice Gail doing the same. I walk over and help wash her hair with the water from my canteen.

"Don't you need the water to clean off?" she asks.

"No, I'm gonna go to the water pipe and clean up there."

"Wait a minute, that's a great idea. I'll get out of these muddy clothes and come with you. I even have some shampoo."

As I pass my tent, I grab a joint and light it. She comes out in a bathrobe, and we head towards the water pipe. I hand her the joint as we walk. She takes a hit, turns, and kisses me blowing the smoke into my mouth. Then I blow it out.

"You know," I say, "the concert is probably gonna go on through the night again, especially since they lost hours of music because of the storm."

"I thought we were gonna make our own music," she says.

With all that went down this weekend, I can't imagine I blushed, but my face seems to feel warm all of a sudden. We don't finish the joint, but hand it off to a couple as we get close to our watering hole.

She removes the robe and stands there naked except for red panties. She bends over to get as much water coming out of the pipe as she can to clean off the mud. She throws handfuls of water on herself, dunks her head under the streaming water, and wets her hair, adding shampoo as she starts washing it. I take off my headband and wring it out, then proceed to get naked and follow her lead. Once we're done we stand facing each other like Adam and Eve and walk slowly towards each other. I'm staring right into her eyes as she's staring back into mine, and I put my arms around her shoulders as her arms wrap around my waist. Now I close my eyes and can feel her breasts against my chest. We kiss as our legs interlock. We're standing completely still while embracing. Then, I feel myself getting stiff against her leg, and she jumps back and says laughingly,

"Put that thing away."

"I wonder if that's what Adam heard Eve say?" I questioned.

Then she puts her robe back on and turns her towel into a bun on top of her head. I just wrap my towel around my waist and carry my wet clothes as we walk back hand in hand.

"I was really scared," she says, "when I saw the black sky heading towards us. I didn't know what to do. I didn't know what to think."

"I probably would have been really scared of the sky too, but I didn't have time to think. The look on your face is what scared me and I just went into safety mode, and wanted to protect you."

"I felt safe with you," she says.

"As if I could really do anything."

"You did, you really did. Being held by you made me less scared."

"Well, I felt like I had to hold on to something, it might as well have been you. I just wanted you to be safe," I assure her.

"Glenn, You are so sweet. You know this is our last night."

"Don't remind me," I say.

As we continue walking, we come to a clearing where we can see brightness in the sky coming from the direction of the concert, and we could hear the murmur of music.

"Can't make out who that is," she says.

"It's Country Joe and the Fish. They were going on stage when we left."

"So, what was the best part of the weekend?" she asks.

"Meeting you."

"I know that, You Silly. I mean of the concert."

"It was you — "

"Again!"

"Let me finish. It was you . . . cutting through the crowd to take me to see The Who close up. That was far-out."

"I was sure you were gonna say Santana."

"That was good too," I assure her, "but you taking me through the crowd was quite brilliant and being with you for The Who was wonderful. What about you?" What was the best part?

"Hmmm, let me think."

"You can say me."

"When we were getting high, listening to Melanie."

"I wasn't with you during Melanie."

"Oh, right! She says. "That was someone else."

She then runs ahead of me laughing, but I'm right behind her and stop her as we reach my tent.

"Are you tired?" I ask.

"Not so much."

"Okay, then we can go back and hear more music. When I'm ready I'll come and get you."

"You know, Glenn, we can still go to my tent and rest."

She reaches for my hand and pulls me, leading me to her tent. I follow with my damp clothes in my other hand, and I lose myself in the moment, not knowing exactly what's going on. I feel clean, and I feel good, and I feel naked, I mean, I am naked. Tonight's the last night with her and our last night at Woodstock. With that in mind we enter her tent together.

Once inside she puts on a lantern that hangs down from the tent, right over her sleeping bag. It casts a nice dull light within the tent, and she tells me to lie my damp clothes down and to close the flap.

"I thought we're gonna listen to some music?"

"I told you I want to make music . . . with you."

She opens the sleeping bag wide. She removes the towel from her head and then proceeds to remove her robe, and in doing so, exposes her lovely body to me once again. She lays down, naked, on her back with nothing on but a pair of panties and a smile.

Her long hair lies under her head and shoulders this time, not covering her at all. I can actually admire her nakedness, which I do. She's lying so exposed in front of me. There's a nice curvature to her breasts, and they look soft. Her body is beautiful as the dim light casts down from above. She's been a wonderful companion during these last few days, and she's just been amazing. The fact she lets me gaze upon her is crazy to me, but I feel like the luckiest guy at Woodstock.

She arches her back, disrupting my fixation on her and my eyes just naturally look towards her face. Her head is slightly cocked, and her mouth is biting her lower lip, I can tell she wants me to enjoy the view, but not for much longer. My gaze slides down her body. Her waist curves slightly inward till it gets to her hips. Her hands lay on her stomach with her thumbs bent downward and her fingers lay flat on her tummy with her forefingers touching, causing a heart-shaped image with her cute little belly button right in the middle. From below her panties, two slender legs stretch out and continue downward from her hips. I utter softly, "You are breathtaking."

Then she starts patting the left side of the sleeping bag with her left hand, inviting me to lie down next to her as she reaches up and shuts off the lantern.

"Why don't you get rid of that towel and come here and hug me?"

I stand perfectly still except for maybe the slight shaking in my knees, and I unhinge the towel and let it drop. The moon is now casting it's light down on the tent. Although the light in here is just shy of complete darkness, I still manage to find the edge of the sleeping bag and crawl over to Gail.

Our bodies are face to face, and we lean into each other. I slide my left hand over her, and I cup her head. I can feel her nakedness and warmth against my body, and her breath on my cheek. I can smell the scent of the shampoo in her hair.

I want to tell her how much I like her, but it's only in my head as our lips meet. My hand trails down from her head over her shoulder blades. Her skin is so smooth, and it feels so nice as I continue sliding further down over the curvature of her back.

She lies down on her back and my fingers glide gently around to her belly. Our lips never part. I'm slightly over her as I continue touching her belly and moving downward. I can't put my other arm around her because both my right arm and her left arm are sort of trapped between us. My free hand keeps exploring, drifting further down till I touch the top of her panties. She immediately pulls her mouth away and whispers,

"The panties stay on, and nothing goes underneath them."

"I wasn't gonna do anything," I whisper, back; "my hand just slid down."

"On purpose," She accuses.

"Maybe, I don't know, I wasn't even thinking of anything except how nice you feel."

"I don't think you will do anything I don't want you too, but I get a little nervous. Boys always want to go there. I like kissing you, and I love the way you hold me. It makes me feel special."

"You are special," I tell her.

"You're so sweet . . . but anything under my panties are off limits, I'm sorry, I just get scared."

"That's fine." I assure her, "Really, it's fine."

We go back to kissing as I continue roaming back up her belly to her breast. Her free hand is stretching across us holding the back of my neck, as we kiss. I'm purposely taking it slowly because I want her to feel comfortable and I want both of us to enjoy ourselves and remember this night, our last night, forever. My hand follows the curvature of her stomach as it glides slowly across her soft, warm skin. I feel the slight incline as it crosses above her belly button, and now I feel the thin elastic at the top of her underwear again, but immediately change the direction of my hand, sliding along her tummy again resting it upon her breast. I give it a gentle caressing and glide downward again across her stomach. We stop kissing as my hand reaches the elastic. Suddenly her hand grabs my wrist, and everything stops. I can feel her breath on my neck as she whispers, "Only on the outside, nothing underneath, okay?" and then she pushes my hand further down.

I don't answer with words, but my hand glides over her panties, and she seems be at ease with that. My hand goes down her thigh, but soon floats back up and I feel her thighs part slightly. I find my hand going between them, and my fingers rub in a circular motion at the junction between them. I press down firmly on the soft spot that is dead center on the fabric protecting her womanhood. I've been getting excited all this time also as my groin is pushing against her leg. Her thighs clamp my hand in place tightly so I can hardly move it, and her body becomes tense, and I hear a soft moan. Then a gush of dampness seeps out through her panties, soaking my hand, and I can't hold myself back any longer.

Our slight movements stops, and it seems like the whole world stopped. We lay still as her legs relax, loosening the grip on my hand. Her body goes limp, and her head turns away as I feel exhausted and fall over onto my back. I think of what Hugh said early this morning, "We must be in heaven, man." That's the only explanation I have . . . I must be in heaven, man.

August 18, 1969 (Monday)
CHAPTER 24: BS&T CSN&Y

I awake in darkness, and it takes only a split second to remember exactly where I am. It's extremely quiet, and I feel Gail at my side. Her body's limp and I can tell by her breathing that her head is turned away. My arm is asleep under her body, but I slip it out without disturbing her.

I search for my clothes in the darkness, and they're right where I put them. I mean, why wouldn't they be? They are still a little damp, so I pick them up and tiptoe outside carrying them. It's dark outside the tent as well, but there are a half dozen hippies sitting around the campfire, and the light is enough to guide me to my tent. I cover my nakedness with my clothes and can hear the faint sound of music in the background as I enter my empty tent.

A few minutes later I'm clean and come out in dry clothes. I walk over to the fire, sit down with the others and ask for the time. One tells me it's about 1 a.m., so it's Monday. We talk about the afternoon, and I'm told that a lot of people left during and well after the terrible storm.

I can see Gail's tent light up and remember how the sunlight cast an orange hue within the dark tent yesterday, but tonight the orange hue is transmitting outward from the canvas. With very little light anywhere else on Groovy Way, it lights up the darkness, which only makes it easier to get back to her.

I approach her tent, and I can see her at the opening. She's halfway out, and I can see she's still naked. As I get closer she comes out to gives me a nice short kiss on my cheek. She says it's chilly and she wants to clean up so we can go back to the concert, then she turns around and scurries back to her tent. I can see her red panties as the light cast out from her tent when she opens the flap, then she disappears inside.

After a few minutes I knock on the tent knowing there is no sound, it's just an inside joke to myself.

"How you doing in there?" I ask, not wanting to just bust in. "Can I enter?"

"Of course you can, You Silly."

I open the flap as I say, "I was just being polite."

"You are so considerate."

"I try."

"I know you do. I'm almost ready."

She's standing there in a reddish-purple tie-dye blouse with blue at the bottom and blue at the sleeves. My eyes trail down from the blouse past her naked legs to her bare feet. As I stare back up she's twirling my red bandana around one finger.

"I believe this is yours," she says.

"I wondered where that went. I knew I dropped it somewhere when I was carrying my clothes."

She tosses it over to me, and I immediately place it back on my head even though it's still slightly damp, and I notice she's wearing a headband with multi-colors and also my bracelet.

"I can see you're not quite ready." I say.

She doesn't answer, but it really wasn't a question. Then she asks me if I'm hungry. It seems to me we are always talking about eating. It must be from all the pot smoking.

"I guess I am," I reply.

"Why don't you wait by the fire and I'll finish getting dressed and bring something out soon?"

"No brownie, I insist."

"No brownies, they're long gone."

About 15 minutes later Gail comes out of her tent with a couple of bowls of cereal. She has on torn jeans, and has put a sweater on over the blouse, and she has different moccasins on. As we sit at the fire with the other hippies, they light up and begin passing the joint around. I would usually take a hit and pass it to Gail, but I don't want any right now. Gail notices, and she also declines. Oddly, turning down a joint is a reaction I don't remember either of us doing this whole weekend except when we ate the brownie, but we chose to decline now. I can only guess for myself that I just want to be straight these last few hours with Gail. I hope that is her reason for saying "no" as well.

When we finish eating the cereal I go in my tent to get my jacket as she places the bowls in her tent and grabs her sleeping bag. I take it from her to carry as we head towards the field. I take her hand, and we walk around the cornfield till we come to the spot where we sat the first night together. There are a few hippies sitting back here because it's higher ground: no puddles, and less mud.

I can see the major crowd of people still in front of the stage half way back, but so many have left that there a huge gap from that crowd to the mob that sits around the back edge of The Bowl.

There were far less people at the stage the first night, but so many more last night. The hippies at the campfire were correct; a lot of concertgoers have left. I put down the sleeping bag, turn to Gail and put my arms around her waist. She does the same to me as she snuggles her head into my chest. We just hold each other firmly without uttering a word. I'm facing the stage and just staring out. "What a hell of a weekend," I think to myself, not wanting to break the silence between us. I can see the spotlight on the stage as the group breaks the silence with their song. The first lyrics tell me the group is Blood, Sweat and Tears, and as the song continues I hold her and sing softly to her,

> *"I choose you for the one*
> *Now we're havin' so much fun*
> *You treated me so kind*
> *I'm about to lose my mind*
>
> *You made me so very happy*
> *I'm so glad you*
> *Came into my life"*

She's so comfortable to hold and she doesn't move, but I know she's listening to my every word.

> *"The others were untrue*
> *But when it came to lovin' you*
> *I'd spend my whole life with you*
>
> *Cause you came and you took control*
> *You touched my very soul*
> *You always show me that*
> *Lovin' you is where it's at*
>
> *You made me so very happy*
> *I'm so glad you*
> *Came into my life*
>
> *Thank you, baby"*

174

She lets go of me, and it looks like she's crying, but she turns away quickly. I stop singing and she's wiping her eyes.

"Are you alright?" I ask.

She turns back to me.

"Yes, I'm fine."

"Gail?"

"Yes, Glenn?"

"I haven't known you very long — "

"Stop right there!" she insists.

"Here we go again, you know, Gail." I say. "You stop me every time I want to tell you how I feel."

"That's because I know what you're gonna say."

"Yeah, perhaps you do, but — "

"I know and I don't want to hear it. I don't want to hear anything foolish. I want what we have . . . here . . . now. Can't we just enjoy it and not ruin it?"

"You think what I might say may ruin it all?"

"It couldn't ruin it till now," she says. "It's been wonderful, fun and very exciting. The weekend's been terrific, but it just might ruin it from this point on."

"That's why you always stop me?"

"In a simple word, "Yes.""

"But . . . "

"I'm sorry Glenn, there are no buts, except this butt."

She turns around and bumps me with her butt and the tension seems to be broken, at least for the time being.

"And" I add, "it's a beautiful butt at that.

"I'd like to think so, and I'm gonna plant it right here."

She picks up the sleeping bag, folds it over a few times, and places it on the damp ground for us to sit on. We sit close together, and I think to myself, "No! I don't want to ruin this."

"You are pretty incredible, she says as if to comfort me. "I mean that in a good way."

"What other way could I possibly take that?"

"No other way."

"Gail, I have a question. Why did you pee all over yourself and me in the tent?"

"Really?" she asks. "That's what you want to know? You are so naïve."

"Why do you say that?"

She repeats, "You are pretty incredible, but pretty naïve too."

Then she kisses me, short and sweet and on the cheek.

"For someone so naïve, you sure rock my world."

"I don't think I'm naïve. I guess you just got so excited you couldn't help yourself, right?

"Yep! Gail confesses. "That's it."

Blood, Sweat and Tears end their set. We just chat as we cuddle and keep ourselves warm. We found out from hippies around us that we have missed Ten Years After, an English group with a very talented guitarist named Alvin Lee. The Band, a group that had toured with Bob Dylan the year before, and Johnny Winter, who was joined by his brother Edgar. And then,

> "Ladies and gentlemen, please welcome with us, Crosby, Stills and Nash and Young!"

"Crosby, Stills, Nash and Young, WOW! I'm glad we didn't miss them," I say.

They start with "Judy Blue Eyes," and when they finish the song David Crosby speaks into the microphone, "This is our second gig."

> Steven Stills takes over, "This is only the second time we've ever played in front of people, man, we're scared shitless."

They go into "Blackbird," as Nash tries to shush the audience because it's a much quieter song and the audience is still applauding from the last one, and then their harmony fills the air. It's beautiful music to listen to at 3:00 a. m., especially with my arm around Gail. This is their acoustic set and they also sing "Helplessly Hoping" and "Marrakesh Express." We don't even realize that Neil Young isn't on stage until he comes out to join them for the electric guitar set which includes "Long Time Gone" and "Wooden Ships." Neil is very annoyed with the cameraman filming right up in his face and is shooing him away.

When they finish it's about 4:00 a.m., and we spread out the sleeping bag so we can lie down, and as we do we tend to doze off. Then at one point we both wake up to what is no surprise, but is indeed astonishing.

CHAPTER 25: Sunrise

We both sit up and face the east to see the most magnificent sky so far, the light slowly casting over the landscape. The sun isn't peeking over the horizon yet, but its morning light is reflecting off the clouds in the sky announcing to everyone that a new day is beginning. The few clouds in the far distance cast an orange hue on top, working down to a bright yellow color underneath. I swear I see light pinkish rays that seem to reach up spreading outward just seconds before a slice of the sun appears, and I'm not the only one who sees it. There is an exciting murmur from everyone. Now more of the sun appears, and if you concentrate on it being a fixed object in the sky, you can actually see the earth moving to expose its brilliance. Now the orange fades outward as the bright yellow sun illuminates the sky. Once it steps above the line, the light show is over and the day is here, and it looks like it's gonna be a good one, except for the one thought in the back of my mind – it's our last day.

The show is over, and as I look over the field, I can see the crowd that still remains. The ground itself looks like a battlefield, and I, as well as all who are still here, have lived through the battle. The field is no longer green. It's brown with patches of mud and muck stretching across this landscape. Luckily we are up on this ridge, and the ground is only damp. I can see small groups maneuvering their way cautiously across the terrain between the still waters, while others just walk straight through them. I can see others sitting on the ground between the little streams that developed during the storm. People are twisting their blankets in an attempt to wring out the water. Others are milling around, talking, smiling, and laughing. I look at Gail, and we smile at each other because we made it through the storm just like they did.

I look out and continue to see more people walking across the swamp-like field that now leads to the stage. Most wearing jackets or sweaters and whatever clothes they have left to help keep them warm because the morning air is still holding a chill. Plastic ponchos are also being worn, handmade from the plastic sheets we used as floor coverings earlier.

On the ground are scattered clothes, every kind imaginable – shoes, socks, shirts, hats, pants and even underwear. Blankets just left in their place, next to bottles, cans, and cigarette packs. Anything water can destroy it did, and water can destroy anything. The muddy scenery is also filled with trash, the likes of paper plates, cups and plastic utensils, broken umbrellas, and small bags of garbage.

It's 6 in the morning and all of a sudden the speakers are alive again and wastes no time,

"Ladies and Gentlemen, Paul Butterfield!"

It's hard to believe the show is gonna continue. The main crowd is close to the stage, but the other devoted fans are scattered throughout the field, sitting wherever they feel comfortable. We decide to leave to see what we can scrounge up from what's left at our campsite for breakfast. When we get there Brian and Sam have just finished eating and tells us we can have the last of everything. That's great, we have no eggs, and just the ends of the bread, and four slices of cheese, and all the cooking utensils we need. As they head to the field, Brian says, "Eat what you want and throw the rest away." He also adds, "I'm hoping to leave by noon."

Gail goes to see what she can scrounge up, and finds a box of cereal, maybe enough for two bowls, but nothing left to drink except water. We eat what's left and throw the empties away. As we head back to the concert seats, we hear the sound of blues filling the air and a harmonica being played by Paul Butterfield himself. The sun is strong, and it's starting to warm up the people and dry up the field.

CHAPTER 26: Feeling the Blues

As we sit back down, what runs through my mind are Brian's last words, "hoping to leave by noon," I hated hearing those words, and I'm really gonna hate doing them. The best part of this weekend is that I met Gail, and she's just amazing. I have to face the fact that I will probably never see her again and try not to be sad about it. The way I'm trying to do that is to keep in mind that I have a lot more living to do and there's so much more in store for me. If I can experience something like this at 19, then my future should look bright. I will just keep this weekend as a fond memory and look forward to many more concerts and many more girls like Gail. Maybe she's right, not that I shouldn't let my feelings out, which she doesn't let me do anyway, but rather to not have feelings like this in such a short time. After all, we just met. These thoughts will help me be brave for the goodbyes that will surely come, according to Brian, "before noon."

"Gail, I haven't asked you before, but how are you getting home?"

"I have a ride," She answers.

"Oh . . . good. Will you need help with your tent?"

"No, it's not really mine, and I'm just gonna leave it."

"Well, you know it's really been great here . . . with you. I'm gonna miss you. Maybe you can give me your number and—"

"I don't know," she says, stopping me in my tracks.

"You know," I continue, "it's been so surreal; the music, the people, sharing this weekend with you. Maybe I should just chalk it up to a great experience."

I'm trying to show her I'm comfortable with her answer.

"Oh, that's really a good idea," she says.

"Well, I . . . I don't have much of a choice do I."

There goes my cover, trying to show her how cool I am and caving in on the very next sentence.

"Oh you'll be fine," she says, "it's a summer fling, all wrapped up in one weekend."

"Yeah, but I thought I left that at my summer camp."

"What do you mean?"

"Nothing, nothing at all."

"You're upset."

"No, I just feel . . . funny, sad, maybe . . . empty."

"Well, I think your upset. I can see it in your voice and hear it in your face."

"What?"

"I'm just trying to make you laugh," she says.

"By hearing it in my face and seeing it in my voice?"

"Yeah! Come on, that's funny. Don't be such a downer. I'll make you eat another brownie."

"No, anything, but that. Wait," I say, "that wasn't so bad."

"Okay, you're starting to sound better," she says.

"For now."

Then we hear the music of Paul Butterfield as he is whalin',

> *"Yeaaah Baby, every thing's gonna be alright!*
> *OHH OHH OH, Every thing's gonna be alright,*
> *You wait till tomorrow morning now, gonna battle through*
> *the night.*
> *Tell ya baby, don't ya wanna man like me, OH, yeah, yeah,*
> *yeah, don't you wanna man like me, now? Owww!"*

"Yeah baby," I sing, "don't you want a man like me?"

"Stop that now or I'm leaving," she said quite angrily.

She sounds a bit serious, but then I notice what appears to be a tear just before she turns her head away. Her hand goes up to her face, and I can only imagine she's brushing it away. As she turns back, I can see her glossy eyes, and the sad look on her face. Of course, the glossy eyes I've seen all weekend, but the sad look, that's new. Then she squints her eyes, and I can see what appears to be a teardrop running down her cheek, as she tries to hide it by looking away again.

"Oh, babe, don't cry," I say.

"I'm not!" she snaps back. Then swinging her hand aimlessly at me, saying, "Get away!"

I don't recognize this face, and I don't want to see it now. All weekend I saw a smiley face, a laughing face, a stoned face and just before the storm, a frightened face. These are the only looks I want to remember seeing. Not this sad one, especially if I'm the cause. She turns away and looks towards the stage so I can't see her face. I step close to her, and I put one arm around her.

"You're gonna ruin your make-up," I say.

Then she pushes my arm off her.

"I don't wear any make-up!"

"Then how about if you and I just make up?" I ask.

She starts to grin and turns to me and hugs me tightly while burying her face into my shoulder. I think she's really trying to dry her eyes on my jacket. I hear her say something under her breath, it's unclear, but I take a guess and respond hoping I'm right. "Yeah, I'm gonna miss you too."

CHAPTER 27: The Last Groups

We don't say another word during the break, the longest silence we've had the whole weekend. At first, she just stands there while I try comforting her by gentle rubbing her back. Then, we both sit down, but she's not ready to make eye contact yet, and I'm not forcing the issue. Then the silence is broken,

> *"Sha Na Na Na, Na Na Na Na Na, Get a job,*
> *Sha Na Na Na, Na Na Na Na Na. Get a job."*

"Please Ladies and Gentlemen, Sha Na Na!"

She stands up and looks at me, and I can see her eyes are a little swollen.

"I didn't mean to make you cry," I say.

"I wasn't crying," she says. "Now be quiet, and let's dance."

She pulls me up off the ground.

We start dancing to that '50s sound of early Rock & Roll by Sha Na Na. We're smiling and laughing again. Do we have to go through every damn emotion this weekend? We dance wildly to "Jailhouse Rock," "Whip Out," "At the Hop," and even "Teen Angel," a slow one. Of course, we both sing, "Who Wrote the Book of Love?" I wouldn't say it out loud, I wouldn't dare, but I think I'm really falling for Gail in a big way. She would kill me or worse, just walk away without saying goodbye. Anyway, Sha Na Na does a half hour set, but their songs are all short.

Sha Na Na is the group that is probably the most out of place at this concert, but their appearance in the film, Woodstock," sparked a new look at the nostalgic '50's, and inspired the Broadway show, *Grease,* the feature film, *American Graffiti*, and the TV Show *Happy Days*.

There isn't a cloud in the sky, but the sun alone can't fully dry Festival Field. We decide to venture to the stage by maneuvering ourselves through the mud, around the puddles and over the garbage, as we hold hands. Since everyone is standing, we slowly and strategically work ourselves to the front of stage not knowing who would be on next. Boy, were we in for a surprise.

"Ladies and Gentlemen, The Jimi Hendrix Experience!"

"NO FREAKIN' WAY!" Gail screams.

What's left of the crowd roars, all 30,000 of us. He comes on the stage wearing blue jeans, a white, fringed jacket, and a pinkish headband. He goes directly to the microphone and says, in the only the way Jimi's voice can,

> "I want to get it straight, we are tired of the Experience Gypsies, so we want to turn it around and call ourselves Sun and Rainbows, but for short, it's nothing but a Band of Gypsies. Billy Cox, bass, Larry Lee, guitar, Jimba, congas, Mitch Mitchell, drums, Jerry Miller, congas too."

Gail and I rock out like the rest of the crowd to "Foxy Lady," "Fire," and "Purple Haze," to name a few. The music is electrifying, and the heavy smell of marijuana is back in the air. I guess not everything got wet. Jimi makes sure everyone is wide-awake by playing his famous rendition of "The Star Spangled Banner." He ends his set and the concert with "Hey Joe."

No artist at Woodstock was to get more than $15,000, so in order to give Jimi the $30,000 he required, he was booked as two acts, one for an acoustical set and one for an electrical set, each at $15,000.

He was the highest paid performer of the show. It should also be noted he and his manager demanded he play last because they felt the star of any show always plays last. Jimi could have been in for a very big surprise because Michael Lang wanted country singer Roy Rogers to close the show by singing the song he is most identified with, "Happy Trails To You." Rogers' manager said definitely not and Roy himself later said, "I probably would have been booed off the stage by all those goddam Hippies."

Jimi ends his set right after 11:00 a.m. Chip approaches the microphone for the last time, bringing an end to the festival,

"Good wishes, good day, and a good life."

The sound in the air ceases, and the silence is somewhat eerie. The speakers have gone silent before, but this time it's different, this time it's over. There aren't any more introductions, warnings, or announcements. The crowd is dispersing, but many hippies are cleaning up the garbage and putting it in piles throughout the field.

For Gail and myself the concert is officially over, and very soon it will be officially over for us as well. We walk back to the campsite trying to avoid the mud as best we can. As we reach the cornfield, I tell her I will be a minute and go to water the corn stalks for the last time.

When I finish, I decide to look one more time at The Bowl that held the greatest Rock & Roll event of all time. There are quite a number of people still roaming, cleaning up the remains. I see they have created a huge peace sign made of the debris. It's symbolic of both the chaos of the weekend and the peace. I throw a kiss to the stage, "Goodbye."

When I come out of the cornfield, Gail is with Brian and Sam, and once I reach them, I take Gail immediately to the running water from the mysterious pipe to wash the mud off our feet. I see Brian and Sam taking down the tent, so I ask Gail one more time if she's sure she has a ride. She nods and softly says, "Yes." We hold each other tight and kiss lovingly. It's the last kiss, and it will have to be remembered forever. Then we walk past Brian and Sam. She says, "Goodbye," to them and heads to her tent. She wants to go in alone, which is probably a good idea. So I go back and help them gather our belongings until she comes out moments later. She's carrying one bag; her sleeping bag is left on the other side of the cornfield, wet, and not worth saving.

One last quick little peck and away she walks, never looking back. I watch until Sam says, "Enough already. Help us." We each have a bag with clothes, and we also have the cooler, canteens, the tent folded as best we could, and our sleeping bags. I believe we have everything as we head towards the car, which luckily isn't too far away. Well, everything except my heart that I've lost.

"Well, it seems we all had a great time," Brian says.

"Yeah," I reply. "I did, and as great as it was, that's how terrible it is now."

Although, I think to myself, Sharon is waiting for me. I guess I can have Brian drop me off at camp, and finish off the summer with my job and my girl. She's not my girl . . . anymore.

"She's really hot," Brian says of Gail. "You couldn't get her in the real world."

"First of all, this is the real world, and second . . . why not?"

"You're too ugly, man!" Sam says.

"It's all in the timing, the circumstance. It's not like this at home," Brian adds.

"Come on, you got lucky, real lucky." Sam adds. "You probably screwed her a few times, didn't you?".

"You know what? We never screwed."

"What! You never fucked her? No way!" Sam said in disbelief.

"What'd she tell you, she was a virgin?" Brian asks.

"Ahh, you know, it never came up. I don't really know. We had a great time and did lots of things, but no fucking, okay? Now you got me talking like you. She was as naughty as an innocent girl can get."

"Naughty! Innocent!" Brian repeats. "What the heck are you talking about?"

"Never mind," I say. "Just take me home. I'm ready for the summer to be over, I'm leaving this all behind and just want to go back to the Bronx.

As we past a painted bus, I can see our car about four cars away, with a figure leaning on it.

"Is that Gail?" I ask, holding back my excitement.

"Yeah, man, we are just giving you a hard time. She asked if we could drive her to the city. She just didn't want us to tell you," Sam says.

I pick up my pace, to get to the car sooner. She's playing with the bracelet I gave her, and then turns to me as I get there.

"What are you doing here?" I ask.

"Waiting for my ride, You Silly," she says with a big smile on her face.

I look up to the sky, and say, "Thank you."

"Why don't you just thank me?"

So I gladly do, with a kiss.

We put all our crap in the trunk. Brian and Sam sit in the front, and I sit in the back just like the way we came, but I'm bringing home a keeper. The cars move steadily from Yasgur's farm, and soon enough, we find ourselves on State Route 17B to I-87 heading to New York City.

EPILOGUE:
The Aftermath

The aftermath of the concert brought enormous recognition to certain artists like Richie Havens, Santana, and Joe Cocker. It wasn't as much the actual concert as it was the concert film, "Woodstock" which was released just seven months later. The film won an Academy Award for The Best Documentary Feature.

People involved with the filmmaking arrived earlier that week. By Friday night it was felt by some of the camera crew that this event was something special, something more than a rock concert. By Saturday night the media had the whole world watching. Director Michael Wadleigh, because of so many hours of film footage, used split screen technology, and in that way was able to show as much of the audience and the on goings off-stage as well as the magnificent performances on-stage. He was able to re-create, at least on film, the Woodstock experience and that is the number one reason after almost 5 decades, that this is still an important event and not just a footnote in history. This masterpiece continues to remind all who were there, that it really happened. It shows our generation, that in the sixties anything was possible, and shows all born since then, that it did happen; the greatest peaceful event in history.

It was made famous not only because of the unbelievable musical artists, but even more so, by the people. Let's not forget Woodstock Ventures Inc., and their contribution of throwing the whole damn party, but there should be something also mentioned about mankind, I just couldn't think of a way to phrase it.

The idea to film the event was Artie Kornfeld's and even John Roberts was skeptical because documentaries very rarely make money. But Artie had a great argument. He said, "Many think this festival is going to cause a giant riot. If it does you'll have the biggest disaster film in history, and we'll all make money." So they went for it and it's a good thing they did because Woodstock Ventures Inc. sold the rights to Warner Brothers for over a million dollars, which helped take a big bite out of their debt. However, John Roberts said he wasn't out of debt till 1980. I want to make you aware that there was no merchandising at this event. No T-shirts, key chains, cups, posters, or anything else for sale. Tickets were pre-sold, and no money for tickets was collected at the concert. Programs were eventually thrown away in boxes. There was no souvenir to show you had been at Woodstock. You just held on to the experience and had your story. This is my story.

I must add my own take here by saying that the two promoters of Woodstock Ventures Inc., John and Joel could have declared bankruptcy. They did not, but they continued to pay for the clean up of Yasgur's farm. They also honored ticket returns to the buyers who sent back their tickets because they didn't get into the area to see the concert (who could tell whether the people actually got in or not?) I, for one, got in, didn't return my ticket, still have my ticket, and admire John Roberts and Joel Rosenman. They showed tremendous character and for that I call each one, a *mensch*. That's not to say I leave out Artie Kornfeld and Michael Lang. In fact, I hope they all get inducted into the Rock & Roll Hall of Fame. I know there is a petition out there recommending it, because I signed it. Let's forgive them for telling a fib. They said they expected 50,000 people coming to the concert, but we now know that they had already sold 180,000 tickets in advance.

To give you the sense of the performance power that graced the Woodstock stage, over one-third of the 31 solo performers or groups that played have been inducted into the Rock & Roll Hall of Fame already, and more are expected to be honored. The first was The Who back in 1990 and the last one was The Paul Butterfield Blues Band in 2015.

Regardless of the few residents that were selling water, the town people had the same spirit as the hippies that came to Yasgur's Farm. Many of the other farmers and residents in the surrounding communities provided food and water. Hospitals and schools opened their doors to provide shelter for the concertgoers. There was also a Jewish Community Center that, hearing of the food shortage, made sandwiches with 200 loaves of bread and 40 pounds of cold cuts, not to mention the two gallons of pickles which I might add were distributed by nuns. This was a remarkable event that will forever be one of the biggest highlights of my life.

You probably want to know about Gail and myself? But before that, just let me say I lost contact with Brian and Sam, although I will always remember they were there with me. Gail stayed with me the rest of the summer, which was nearly over, and went to Syracuse University in upstate New York. She majored in psychology and after grad school set up a practice. She works with children as a child psychologist and went on to have two children of her own, Erin and Rachel and she's living a happy life.

I went to work as an apprentice for my father installing tin ceilings. I now live in Houston, Texas, and manufacture tin ceilings and ship them all over the world. I have two children close to being in there 30s and both know I was at Woodstock and that I'm writing this book. Their names are Erin and Rachel. Yes, the same two children as Gail because we are still together after all these years. We are living in the tradition of Woodstock, which is of peace and love.

In all that time we dated, she would always reinforce that she didn't want me to ruin what we have, so for the most part I listened. I managed to tell her, "I like you, and I like you very much." It took her a while to accept my affectionate words, but I stayed away from telling her anything more. You may find this hard to believe, but Gail actually was the first to say, "I love you" to me. Very soon after, I asked her to marry me, her response, "It's about time."

We still go to many concerts and still see the veteran musicians of Woodstock. Lately we've seen Crosby, Stills and Nash. We saw Santana, who actually had a clip from the *Woodstock* movie when he came out to do his encore, and he played my favorite song, "Soul Sacrifice." Lastly, we recently saw John Sebastian, and I talked to him after the show. He told me he meets a lot of people who tried to get to Woodstock, but didn't, and they all have stories too.

We have gone with our daughters to the Woodstock Museum, and there is a peace sign mowed on the lawn on a slight hill in the very spot we sat on. The cornfield, however, is gone, so is the watering pipe, so is the wooded area, but they were there.

I don't know exactly how to end this book because, in a way Woodstock never ended for Gail and myself. The 50th anniversary is just around the corner, 2019, but I remember this short and sweet interview that seems to be the best way as any to end my story.

Maybe it can be summed up this way:

An interviewer asked the Chief of Police what he thought about the kids at the Woodstock Festival.

Chief of Police: "The people of this country should be proud of these kids, not withstanding the way they dress or the way they wear their hair, that's their own business; but their inner workings, their inner selves, their self-demeanor cannot be questioned; they can't be questioned as good American citizens either."

Made in the USA
Middletown, DE
30 January 2017